BANISH THE DEAD

L.C. MARINO

The Haunting of the Whispering House Series

Available in paperback, eBook, and audiobook.

Bury the Child
Burn the Girls
Bless the Mother
Banish the Dead

CONTENTS

This book is dedicated to the mothers who've cried with
the women of the Whispering House along the way.
I hope you've saved a few tears for Mallory and Cora.

ACT 1

THE WAITING

CHAPTER I

ABIGAIL

Abandoned by her family for an eternity among the dead, Abigail stood before the empty clawfoot tub waiting for her dead sister's return.

And the waiting burned.

Waiting can be a punishment, a price to pay for the narcissism and neglectfulness of others. Sometimes people wait because they're left behind, sacrificed for the sake of others. They become the lower priority, a shadow trailing more urgent needs.

Of course, the house didn't care. Its inanimate objects, old furnishings, and dusty decorations sat in their usual spots, decades removed from their placement. No feet shuffled across polished wood floors. No words passed between loved ones. The house was nothing but a box of dead space, its walls containing the void of a bleak history and the brutal promise of a lonely future.

Standing in the upstairs bathroom, Abigail's body craved rest and healing. While her heart seethed, the wounds spanning her wrists throbbed in concert with her pulse, cyclical hints of irritation and possible infection. Bruised muscles and sore bones creaked beneath her skin. Yet, her dead family expected her to demonstrate paramount patience while Constance fulfilled her promise to return and rejoin her sister.

"The future belongs to those who believe in the beauty of their dreams," Abigail said, her raspy voice bouncing off the bathroom's hard surfaces. She used to love that quote from Eleanor Roosevelt. Now it pissed her off. In her youth, she believed in the beauty of dreams. Now she realized she had no earthly dreams to believe in. But she had a craving, a want which seemed to radiate from her core.

She needed her people. She needed their love.

But they were all dead. Moved on.

Now what? Was she supposed to just lie around until her future manifested itself? When would that be?

"No, the future belongs to those who take action." Abigail bent over the tub and gripped the hot water valve in her sore hand. The cold metal knob resisted the pressure of her fingers, then finally turned, spilling frigid water into the clawfoot tub.

Goddamn that tub.

Abigail straightened her tight, weary back, closed her sore eyes, and rolled her head to loosen the tension in her neck. Behind her closed lids, she recalled memories so vivid and surreal in contrast to the stale reality she now inhabited. An addictive allure resided in the previous day's events—a gift yanked from her hands, a rejection from the people she loved most. In that liquid space beyond the coffin's black water, she'd felt a magic, that *craving*.

Resolution. Redemption. Release.

Not this loneliness, despair, and longing.

She'd found something worth dying for in that space just beyond life—a reprieve from a difficult existence. But apparently, she wasn't good enough to keep her gift, not worthy of permanent residence on the other side. At least not in the eyes of her family. She'd tried to join her mother and sister, but they'd rejected her.

"You need to live!" she mocked aloud to the empty bathroom. "It's not your time! Don't do this!"

Gatekeepers—the selfish defenders of eternal life.

Abigail opened her eyes and wiped a dampness from under her raw eyelids. She pressed her fingers into the gradually warming flow pouring from the tub's faucet.

"Good enough." Abigail lifted a tapered rubber plug hanging from the spout, untangled the chain, and pressed the plug into the thirsty drain. With nowhere to go, the warm water steadily deepened in the tub's basin.

"Okay, Constance. Work your new magic. I've done my part. Now come home."

She hoped filling the tub would speed things up and bring Constance forth on demand. Perhaps her sister could sense the tub's eagerness from wherever she stood on the other side, the flow sweeping her up and pulling her to the house, back to her sister. Would she return to the tub with Abigail standing there, watching her water birth like a midwife?

She's not coming back. You know that, don't you? She lied.

Abigail's heart sank further. Was Constance only playing the protective big sister role when she'd insisted Abigail remain behind, or was life truly better than whatever waited in death?

You're being ridiculous. Why would she let you die? If the roles were reversed, you would have done the same. You wouldn't let her die.

Ah, but she had. She'd watched her sister burn and done nothing to stop the flames consuming her. And then she'd lied to Constance for *years* before this house unraveled the deception and stole everything from them.

Again.

But no one's here to stop you now, are they?

No, they weren't. Abigail was finally in command of her destiny again.

Abigail unbuttoned her pants and pushed them into a mound around her feet. Peeling her shirt from her tacky skin, she moved gingerly to avoid further agitating the angry scabs on her wrists and forearms. The cold air raised goosebumps across her exposed body but she didn't care. Discomfort seemed trivial. Soon, she wouldn't worry about feeling uncomfortable ever again.

One foot raised, toes pointing down at the water below.

She'll be here any second now, a timid hopeful voice said from the furthest fold of Abigail's mind.

Abigail's foot hovered above the gradually rising water. She watched for ripples or changes in transparency...anything. The water moved naturally, its heat radiating warmth to her foot as she hovered.

She's never coming back, the louder voice said. *Command your destiny. Dream. Take action.*

Abigail pressed her foot into the water and exhaled the few reservations clinging to her logic.

What do you have to lose? Enter the flow and drink deeply. I'll take care of you.

Abigail's back foot entered the tub next and a foreign magnetism drew her into the water. Her hips entered the bath as an erotic warmth spread like willing petals above her pelvis. She quietly sobbed, watching black tendrils course through the water in rivulets of familiar flow.

Her heavy eyelids slid over her delirious vision. Darkness took her.

You don't need eyes to see in the flow.

"I see."

And she did. Two black hands rose from the liquid and ran up the sides of her shaking neck.

Lydia trembled like you. I almost had her.

"Aunt Lydia made it to the other—"

The water covered her mouth and threatened to fill her nostrils with steaming black effluent.

Abigail gave herself over to the hands, opened her mouth, and did as the voice in her mind commanded.

Abigail drank deeply.

CHAPTER 2

CONSTANCE

Entering the afterlife version of her childhood home felt surreal.

Constance followed her cousin Adeline through the back door and into the kitchen and stopped in awe. The kitchen looked exactly as it had in her youth. A tidy row of ceramic jars lined the kitchen counter. Her mother's dish towel hung just below the farmhouse sink, and several children's drawings clung to the pea green refrigerator door, held in place by clusters of round, dark gray magnets. The smell of recently baked bread and the morning's coffee permeated the air. The crisp scent of lemon wood polish drew her farther into the home. Adeline led her toward the center of the house without expressing the same sense of wonder, her head tipped slightly forward and her blue dress flowing like a dream around her as she quickly approached the stairs. Constance fought the urge to explore the rest of the downstairs and revel in the nostalgia of her childhood home.

"It's disorienting, right?" Adeline asked without looking back.

"Yeah. But it feels like the best dream. I never want to leave." Constance meant it, too. She intended to stay there forever. It's all she and her family ever wanted—to be together in their home, in that magic time of their lives before death pulled them from each other. Now they had forever, together.

Without Abigail, of course. But eventually, time would bring her home as well. Death, the great inevitable destination, brings everyone home eventually.

"Well, as far as I know, we're not going anywhere." Adeline giggled as she swung on the banister and darted up the stairs. Constance mimicked her younger cousin's sprite movements, feeling like a breeze coasting up the stairs rather than an eighteen-year-old on the cusp of her young adult years. Suddenly, the weight of the moment hit her.

They were going back. They were climbing back into that godforsaken tub and *going back*.

Returning to Abigail wasn't a revelation, Constance had intended to do so since she'd left her behind in the

Whispering House. But she'd blocked the reality of their situation in that house from her thoughts in defense. The house they'd left didn't look or feel comforting like this. The house they'd left terrified her. But they had to go back, they had unfinished business. She'd follow Adeline into the water, through both time and death, then back to Abigail. Constance did her best to restrain her emotions but the thought of reentering that tub and commuting across death's chasm to Abigail, back to the cold world she'd moved on from, conflicted Constance. Apprehension presented its bright angst first. Her first experience traveling through the fluid conduit between the worlds had deeply frightened her. The liquid darkness dripped with the venom of death's sting. And now she was willingly reentering that horrible sea of unknown shadows.

You don't have a choice. Abigail needs you.

Fear struck her heart like a swift punch. They'd left Abigail alone in the darkness, in Shadow Mother's nest. Memories of the flooded house, overwhelmed by Shadow Mother's infestation, choked Constance's hopes.

"How did we leave her there like that?"

Abigail was a wounded dove, and they'd tossed her from the nest to fend for herself against a terrifying predator.

I didn't have a choice. She tried to kill herself. I had to save her, even if it meant sending her back to that place.

The memory of finding Abigail in the backyard, in the space between life and death, surfaced in the hurricane of her thoughts. Her sister begged to stay with them, with their family, and Constance had forced her to return to life. She'd been the protector again, the one to stand for what's right. She couldn't allow her sister to choose death over life, even if Abigail couldn't see the logic in living.

"It was the right thing to do. She'll be there," Adeline said.

Reaching the top of the stairs, Constance nearly ran Adeline over when the girl entered the bathroom and suddenly stopped inside the doorway.

"What the heck?" Adeline asked, sounding perplexed.

"What is it?" Constance leaned around her to investigate the tub. Black water filled the tub to the porcelain lip, threatening to spill over to the spotless white tile floor.

"I've always had to fill it before going back. It's never been...waiting for me." Adeline sounded distant in her confusion.

"Do you think–"

"Hurry. Get in," Adeline interrupted before Constance finished her question.

An intoxicating magnetism drew Constance to the water like a familiar hand dragging her over a cliff into a raging sea. She felt compelled by a force on the other side, beckoned to enter the flow and brave the currents between the nightmare of her past and the beauty of her new existence in the afterlife.

Abigail.

Hand-in-hand, Constance and Adeline submerged into the vast dark ocean between life and death. Panic bloomed in Constance's heart as the inky fluid filled her nostrils and rolled over her eyes. Once fully submerged, her need to breathe subsided, the tension bled from her muscles, and she succumbed to an intoxicating calm as the current swept them from the Whispering House into endless darkness.

Constance struggled to make out a school of dark forms darting through the surrounding black waters. They moved too fast for her to make sense of what she saw. The current persisted, specs of light shooting past them in flickering bubbles. Constance felt giddy in the flow, at peace but nervous, as it pulled them toward the living.

Suddenly, Constance felt incredibly small. Adeline gripped her tight and pulled her close as large hulking blooms passed beneath them.

Are those...trees? They can't be. A forest submerged in a vast body of water? How?

The forest canopy passed beneath them in a steady motion. Constance felt like she was flying through an inverted world, water above land, through a sea instead of air.

Were the trees there last time?

Memories of her first trip to the afterlife evaded her. Why couldn't she recall those images? Only the emotion of wonder came to her.

"Enter the flow and drink deeply."

A wet, intoxicating voice rolled through the waters and squirmed into Constance's ears. Adeline's face glowed with fear beside her as if she'd heard the same voice. Then her lips parted and she screamed, her voice dampened by the liquid. Adeline tried to slow them by dragging her hands and feet outside the current, but the flow was too strong.

What's happening? Who's voice was that?

Suddenly she saw it—a tangled mass of black tentacles ahead, knotted and writhing. Beyond the creature, a band of light streamed into the flow from above.

Constance felt their destination in those rays, the house speaking to them, pulling her home.

That mass, terrifying and undulating, appeared closer as it entered an adjacent stream. The ends of the sinking tentacles revealed a form. Long, curling hair and porcelain skin. The tentacles shapeshifted, now arms, the body no longer bulbous, became an ashen gray *woman*.

She's one of us, Constance thought before recognizing her sister's peaceful face.

"Abigail!" Constance screamed in the water, her voice going nowhere.

She swam as hard as she could from the current, entering the pitch-black expanse between the flows. A swarm of dark forms retreated from her like a school of fish evading a predator. They scrambled down into the subterranean canopy of trees beneath them, hiding from the chaos above.

The woods. The ocean. Expansive territories teaming with souls. Somehow the two merged there, the world flooded to its atmosphere.

Adeline and Constance grabbed Abigail and dragged her from the opposing current. A look of recognition filled Abigail's disoriented face. She fought like hell to shed the tentacles curled around her limbs, accidentally clawing at Constance like a drowning woman fighting her rescuer. The approaching band of light pouring through the surface became unbearably bright, blinding them as it pulled them into its source.

Back to the Whispering House. Back to Shadow Mother's nest.

Somewhere in the deep, a woman cried out in anger, her voice muffled by the ocean between life and death.

CHAPTER 3

ABIGAIL

Birthed into light, Abigail collapsed in a tangle of limbs on the cold tile floor. A torrent of water poured from her mouth, followed by a violent fit of coughs echoing off the small bathroom's hard surfaces as she struggled to clear the liquid from her lungs. Her eyes burned, obscuring her vision. Now outside of the flow, back in the frigid air of the house, the briny taste of warm seawater settled on her tongue.

Why did she climb into that goddamn tub?

Her stomach lurched, flipped, and then forced its contents into her throat. She scrambled to the toilet on her hands and knees, barely reaching the porcelain bowl before a substantial column of black water erupted from her. Her burning eyes squeezed shut as she expelled the rancid emulsion, every muscle in her body ridding her of the tepid water filling her stomach and lungs. Abigail gasped for air as the stream of vomit subsided. Shaking and numb, she rolled onto her side on the gritty tile, blinking wildly and coughing to clear her lungs. Relief washed over her. She was alive, free of the water that nearly killed her.

I'm still in you, a velvety voice whispered in her mind. *I am* you now.

Two faceless entities entered her blurry vision and kneeled beside her.

"Give her a minute."

Her cousin Adeline's voice crawled into Abigail's heart and loosened the sutures holding her emotions together. Her sister's voice finished the job, releasing the tears held behind her eyes.

"You're okay, Abbie. I'm back."

Aggressive shivers racked Abigail's waterlogged body as Constance shuffled her into the sitting room. Adeline entered the room behind them carrying old firewood and kindling, presumably from the back porch. She kneeled before the fireplace and stuffed the kindling beneath two expectant logs.

"You're freezing," Constance said. Her eyes scanned the neglected room for a blanket. Water ran from Abigail's clothed body, puddling on the wood floor around her feet.

"The bedsheet. Upstairs–" Abigail choked on her last word, her throat stinging with the sharp tang of bile and salt water.

"Got it." Constance guided Abigail to the floor beside the couch and fled the room to retrieve the sheet.

Abigail's heart throbbed as she watched her sister's ghost leave the room. Constance had kept her promise. She'd come back for her. Maybe everything would be okay after all. Abigail turned her attention to her cousin. The young girl worked quickly to light the kindling in the cool, dormant fireplace.

"I hope these old matches work," Adeline muttered as she fumbled with a long reach wooden match.

She looked so small. So many years had passed since Adeline's death and seeing her now, seeing a *ghost,* so youthful and happy, squeezed sorrow from Abigail's heart.

You poor girl. No one should die so young, she thought, marveling at the depth of Adeline's curls, the porcelain sweep of her neckline, the smooth contours of her exposed cheek. Abigail looked down at the shaking hands tangled in her lap, at her wrinkled skin and broken, misshapen nails. The stark difference between their ages had never been as apparent to Abigail as it did in that moment. A dark, harsh thought emerged in her mind–what if dying young had eternal benefits that dying old couldn't provide? Was it better to live your afterlife as a young soul, forever captured in peak vibrancy and beauty?

Footfalls on the stairs interrupted her thoughts. A moment later, Constance rushed into the room with the sheet partially open between her hands.

"Thanks." Abigail stood to wrap herself.

Constance pushed her hands away, wrapped her in the dingy cotton sheet, and hugged her hard. "I missed you. I told you I wouldn't leave you."

"I wasn't sure you'd come back once you finally crossed over." Abigail choked on the rivaling fear and relief wedged in her throat.

"Are you kidding me? I was coming back no matter how great it is over there."

"Is it? Is it great?" Abigail asked.

Constance pushed back and held her at arm's length. "Death is amazing. But it's not worth dying for."

Abigail heard and accepted the warning in Constance's voice.

"Fair enough. I want to hear all about it." She pulled the sheet tight around her legs and eased back onto the couch, careful not to force a cloud of dust into the air by sitting too hard.

"Not now. Maybe later," Constance replied.

"Jesus, you're still pushy, even after–"

Constance pinched her fingers together in front of Abigail's face, signaling for her to stop talking. She'd been doing that to her for nearly thirty years. While it normally frustrated Abigail, this time it pulled a smile across her lips. She had her sister back.

"I know you're curious, and I'm happy to tell you everything when the time is right. But I'm not sure how long we'll be safe here." Constance leveled her gaze with Abigail's to show her urgency. "Shadow Mother could show herself at any moment."

Sudden, unjustified concern swelled in Abigail's gut. Why did she feel so defensive? An emotional conflict waged in her gradually warming body.

"I don't want to talk about her right now," Abigail snapped.

Constance leaned back a few inches and Adeline turned her head from the small fire growing in the fireplace. She stood without speaking and turned to the sisters sitting on the couch.

"Besides, we don't know who or what she really is," Abigail added. "Maybe *we're* the problem. Maybe you're right and we don't belong here." Abigail felt the venom and contradiction in her words but couldn't stop herself.

Constance's eyes widened, then narrowed, locking with Adeline's. "Let's do this later."

Adeline spoke up. "Constance is right. We don't have much time. We need to tell you about the girl in the woods."

Abigail's anger shifted to a warm tide of excitement. Despite the welcome emotional change, everything felt *off*.

"What girl?"

Constance sat up tall. "We're not sure who she is, but we think she's got something to do with what's happening here. She could be the Shadow Mother for all we know."

Somehow, Abigail knew Constance's assumption was *terribly* wrong. She couldn't understand why or how she knew this, but she did. She closed her eyes and searched her mind for answers but found none. The room swam in her vision as she opened her eyes and refocused on Constance's perfect face in the firelight. She felt like she'd been drinking.

"Tell me about this girl."

CHAPTER 4
CONSTANCE

The early morning winter sky glimmered above them as Constance and Abigail followed Adeline across the backyard. Winter mornings in Virginia often started damp and windy, but on this one, the air was simply bone dry and frigid stillness. Sunlight filtered through thin clouds, casting a bright gray shade across the frosted grass and bare trees. Despite Abigail's badgering, Constance had delayed their adventure until her sister's clothes had dried and her body warmed enough to counter the effects of her liquid rebirth in the upstairs tub.

That damned tub and Shadow Mother had almost taken Abigail. Had almost delivered another of their lineage to premature death. Had Constance been alive and sensitive to her emotions, she would have shivered sympathetically for her sister, but she was all spirit now and realized she'd never physically respond in that way again. She avoided this uncomfortable realization by jumping back into the story of the unidentified girl in the woods.

"Adeline showed me the girl when we were on the other side. There was a grave there I've never seen before. And she lay a few feet away, just inside the treeline–"

"With a baby," Adeline interrupted, apparently eager to spring the story's surprise ending.

"A baby? Are you sure?" Abigail asked. She seemed un-characteristically eager, twisting Constance's curiosity in her direction.

"Yes, we're sure," Constance replied, guiding them across the hard, dormant yard toward the cemetery path. She glimpsed the shed at the edge of her vision and recalled a memory of the doors slowly opening to a swarm of a thousand lightning bugs drifting into the warm summer evening.

So many secrets. Now the world is all strange truths and mysteries, she thought.

"Did she say anything? Did she acknowledge you?" Abigail asked.

"No. She appeared to be sleeping. The baby, too."

"Or dead," Adeline chimed in. "They've been that way forever, as far as the family knows."

"Right...dead in the land of the dead." Constance scoffed. What an odd thing to consider. She supposed she couldn't deny the possibility. After all, none of their relatives had seen the girl move. But she sensed the girl was alive. "Alive in the land of the dead?" she accidentally considered out loud.

"What?" Abigail asked, her face twisted in confusion.

"Nothing. What I'm trying to say is I think she's just sleeping or under some type of spell. But that extra grave. That's got me *very* curious."

The path to the cemetery narrowed around the girls as they descended into the woods. The early dawn light played games with Constance's vision as the gray sky blended with the bare tree canopies and light fog hanging above the earth. Ahead of her, Adeline traversed the path, her youth evident in the playful way she swung her arms as they walked, as if they were strolling through a city park instead of embarking on an early morning graveyard exploration.

Around them, the woods deepened into utter silence. Constance reveled at the difference between traversing the path now and in the afterlife, visions, and dreams before crossing over, spirits whooping and darting in murky shadows between the trees. Now, all stood still.

The woods seemed more *alive* in her visions and after-life, as if death had unlocked a new layer of existence for the departed. She supposed time would prove whether that was a good thing.

Constance's eyes drifted to Abigail's face as they progressed down the path. Her sister seemed deep in thought but also hyperaware and edgy, not her usual upbeat self. Something was up and Constance couldn't put her finger on it.

Can you blame her? She's been through a lot over the past few days.

Her chest ached for Abigail. She'd spent so many years focused on protecting her sister, only to find their roles had been reversed without her knowledge. And that protection came wrapped in a devastating lie, a breach of trust that could have torn them apart had they let it.

"I love you," Constance said, taking Abigail's hand. Abigail feigned a half-hearted smile and blinked away whatever occupied her thoughts. "Are my hands cold when you touch them?"

Abigail answered without hesitation. "Yes. But they've felt that way since you died twenty years ago."

Constance instinctively recoiled and pulled her hand, but Abigail squeezed it tighter. She wanted to say something witty to counter Abigail's blunt response, but she couldn't think clearly as they entered the cemetery. Biting her tongue, Constance guided them between rows of headstones toward the edge of the woods where the girl's body should have been.

"So, nothing's changed," Constance said.

"I look for her every time I come back but she's never here," Adeline replied.

Constance thought about Adeline's wet footprints in the hall and down the stairs each night she'd returned to search for lost loved ones. How many times had she gone to the cemetery to check this very spot? A small voice above them broke her train of thought. She looked up and saw a tiny black body flying across the opening of the trees above them. Constance's eyes lingered on the clouds for another moment before Abigail spoke.

"So, where do you think she is now?"

Adeline pointed behind them to the empty length of dead grass between the woods and the closest grave. "That's where the grave is on the other side. Maybe in there."

Constance and Abigail craned their necks in unison to see where she pointed.

"There's only one way to find out," Abigail said.

Constance groaned.

CHAPTER 5

ABIGAIL

The first plunge of the shovel drove a bone jarring shock through Abigail's fatigued arms. She'd expected the earth to be hard from the evening freeze but she hadn't expected so much resistance. To make matters worse, exhaustion and hunger were finally overcoming her adrenaline.

"I can do this," she said between labored breaths.

Constance placed a supportive hand on her shoulder. "Let's come back later. You need food and rest."

Abigail shrugged her sister's dead hand from her shoulder and lifted the shovel higher in both hands. She closed her eyes and drove it downward with all her strength, imagining the spade pushing beyond the earth's surface. Another bolt of energy shot through her weary hands and up her arms as the shovel's blade met its mark. Abigail opened her eyes and found the shovel embedded a few more inches this time.

"See? I just need to keep going."

"Let her go if she wants," Adeline said from her perch above the neighboring headstone. Somewhere in the woods to their right, a small animal, most likely a squirrel, scurried through crackling leaves as it fled the action in the clearing.

"Don't encourage her. She's exhausted," Constance re-buffed.

"You don't believe I can do it. You've always thought I was weaker than you. Well, now I'm the only one left who can do this." Abigail dumped the meager contents from the shovel, pinched her blueing lips together, and repeated the downward strike. This time, the shovel found more purchase.

Abigail stepped onto the shovel, driving it another few inches deeper. Standing on the shovel's blade, she bounced on both feet and lost her balance, stumbling backward before regaining her footing. Adeline stifled a fit of laughter.

"Who taught you how to use a shovel?" Constance asked, her lips contorting as she fought back a smile.

"You did!" Abigail steadied her feet and lifted the shovel again. As she raised her eyes to her hands, she spotted the dark bird circling the sky above them again. Another joined in the motion.

Two more flew in from the south.

"What's wrong?" Adeline asked, twisting to inspect the sky.

"Starlings," Constance said.

Plink

The girls lowered their faces, exchanged curious looks, then lowered their eyes to the ground in search of the sound.

Plink plink

Abigail felt the grass pulse beneath her feet.

"*What* is–"

"Look!" Abigail jumped from the headstone and pointed at the shovel.

Plink plink plink plink

Abigail and Constance leaned forward to look at the ground. Their heads nearly touched when Abigail saw it.

A long, dark beak poked from the ground, rapping its morse code on the metal blade penetrating the soil.

Plink plink plink plink plink plink plink

Abigail yanked the shovel from the earth and tossed it aside, her eyes glued to the beak frantically searching the air.

"What should I do?"

Jerky unnatural movement haunted the edge of Abigail's vision. She snapped her head up, a chilled vein of fear coursing down her spine. Before her, rigid as boards, Constance and Abigail stood like statues, arms extended and fingers splayed toward the ground. Their eyes went black, their faces turned up to the sky. Their mouths fell open.

Billowing black clouds obscured the winter sky above the circling birds as a sour, smoky wind whipped the treetops into a dance. A shadow fell across the cemetery and the skies turned dark, darker, night.

Abigail looked down in a panic, her feet frozen a mile beneath her scrambling mind. She barely saw the beak spinning wildly in the grass, chirping and crying out as the bare trees groaned in the freezing storm winds.

She tried to reach for her sister, to run, to do *something,* but her eyes remained fixed on the beak, her body no longer under her control. Her knees went soft, then buckled, spilling her toward the screeching beak, onto the frozen cemetery ground. She screamed as she fell but the sound came from somewhere else, somewhere it simply *shouldn't be.*

Her scream spilled from the open, frozen mouths of her sister and cousin.

Impact. Hands and knees. The snapping beak just below her face.

Abigail tried to move but had lost all control of her faculties. But she saw *everything*.

She saw the beak stop spinning in the soil, then close. Her right hand lifted from the ground in a strained claw. Wet soil and grass clippings stuck to her pale fingers as they shook, muscles and tendons straining. Those fingers opened wide above the beak, then lowered until the beak emerged in the web between her thumb and forefinger.

"No! No! No! No! No!" Her screams came in short blasts from Constance and Adeline.

She watched her hand press into the soil up to her wrist as if it were recently turned and loose. That hand squeezed around a feathered body just beneath the surface. The starling's heart pounded like a runaway engine against her palm.

The hand emerged, dirt falling away from the starling's feathers, its eyes blazing in its small skull.

Constance and Adeline fell to their hands and knees beside her, mouths still screaming, their blackened eyes impenetrable windows. Then, driven by some external force, all three of them began digging. Abigail holding the starling in one hand and plying earth with the other.

Abigail's mind fell backward, to another time, to another *mind*–behind another set of eyes.

She no longer saw the starling in her hand or her sister and cousin.

Nor did she hear the screams, the wind, or her own labored breaths.

She no longer dug nearly frozen soil.

Her hands moved under a new power. Love propelled them. Love powered her heart.

She dug with *Lydia's* hands, with *Lydia's* heart.

Her thoughts spun to the aching possibility of reunion, to the love of a precious child lying in wait beneath her.

My God, I'm with Lydia in that moment before her death, Abigail realized in a panic.

But she couldn't stop.

Time looped with every handful of soil the girls removed from the unmarked grave.

In the infallible darkness, Abigail imagined moist clay staining her clothes. She imagined seeing her aching hands and broken nails. None of that stopped her from digging until the wounds on her wrists opened, spilling her blood to the mire. Her hands clawed at the grave in an endless cycle.

She imagined the moon journeying across the night sky as they worked, the silent storm raging around them. She envisioned an impressive field of stars charging an open, clear dome above them and shadows moving between the trees in feral anticipation, sprite spirits thrilled for the girls to find their macabre gift.

Abigail never tired, cramped, or became winded. Lydia's force powered her until her fingers struck hard wood.

Her hands scurried across the stained surface of a rudely constructed pine box, pushing away loose dirt and rock and scooping a channel around one edge in the bordering clay bed.

Above her, in the expansive dark beyond this shallow grave, voices howled and wings flapped in a surging tide of sound. Abigail's heart swelled, spurred on by the wild voices and the pending reunion with what—*who*—she'd unearthed.

Abigail scurried blindly across the lid and up the shallow walls, past Constance's and Adeline's frozen, crouched forms, and toward those howling voices. As she stood upright, stretching her body into the active void above them, she drew a deep, restorative breath, the mineral-rich smell of freshly dug clay and winter woodland flooding her lungs. A murmuration of starlings beat the air inches above her from tree line to tree line, the night a shapeless, undulating sea of broken wings.

Abigail turned her face down to the grave and began to sob. She felt anger and desperation, fear and grief. A vein of confusion ran through it all. Was this the girl from the woods Constance and Adeline told her about?

Abigail took one last deep breath and crawled back into the grave. She wedged her legs between the box and the earth and worked her fingers beneath the lid. She looked back to Constance and Adeline, catatonic in their silent terror. They offered no contest. Pleading words never fell from their open mouths. They waited for the end of this madness. Abigail imagined they all did. The torment of the past twenty years needed to end. A fitting sunset to a nightmare none of them controlled. She closed her eyes and prayed whoever lay beneath the lid would help them resolve their pain forever. Reunite them in peace rather than fear.

End this grief, these visions, this curse. Be our healing whisper.

The box spoke as nails groaned free from their positions. Boards moved. Abigail froze, eyes wide like twin moons, her panting breaths misting the air between her and her new discovery.

A teenage girl lay beneath the boards, a dead starling clutched under one arm.

Abigail's numb hands moved at the end of someone else's arms. Inside her panting chest, a mother's heart broke under a century of grief. She no longer witnessed the world through the eyes of a daughter. The last board quivered in her motherly hands.

"Cora." The girl's name poured from her lips like heavy cream.

The clutched starling's eyes opened. Cora's mouth twitched. The starling stirred.

"Cora, baby." Abigail sobbed uncontrollably. A lifetime of someone else's memories pounded at the edge of her mind, trying to force their way in.

Starlings dropped from the sky one by one, perching on the girl's exposed lower legs, blanketed her thighs, and took position along the edge of the coffin. Abigail tried to wave them away but where she succeeded another filled the void.

"Mother?"

Abigail froze, her eyes glued to the growing ranks of starlings filling the gaping hole in the earth. She grasped for mental control in the madness. *Constance will protect you.* She looked for Constance and Adeline and found them as she'd left them, useless statues trapped in nightmarish form at the foot of the grave.

"Mother."

Don't look. You imagined her voice. This is all a dream. You're still asleep in the closet waiting for Constance to return. But she won't because none of this is real. This house, this grave, this girl, this curse, these ghosts I've lived with my entire life, none of them real.

Cora sat up in the periphery of her vision.

Abigail's pulse pounded so hard spots filled her sight. Sobbing harder, her eyes locked with Constance's black stare.

"Please, Connie."

Ivory fingers reached into view. She had to look, Constance couldn't save her. This was on her.

Abigail slowly turned her head in Cora's direction, her eyes crawling across the inches of terror between them.

Cora's fingers hovered an inch from Abigail's face. The reaching hand at the end of the supple ghostly arm led Abigail to Cora's blinking grit-filled eyes.

Abigail gripped her fleeting sanity with one final thought.

She's just another ghost.

Cora opened her mouth to speak. "See."

Blinding light stole Abigail from the grave, from the feverish world, as Cora's fingers landed on her cheek.

ACT II

1886

CHAPTER 6

CORA

Swaying precariously on one shaky knee in the moist earth of Mother's garden, Cora balanced on a knife edge of pain for seconds that felt like years. She'd spent the morning under the sun, tilling, weeding, and feeding the soil nurturing the vegetable garden. Dehydrated and shaky with insatiable hunger, she needed rest in the back porch's shade. However, when she tried to stand, a debilitating bolt of pain snatched the breath from her lungs and the strength from her trembling thighs. An equally intense wave of nausea swept over her as she dropped to her hands and knees among the green bean sprouts and tomato plants.

Cora squinted against the agonizing pain and tried calling out for Mother, but her empty lungs kept her silent. Her right hand left the garden soil for her bulbous belly.

No movement from the baby. Her fingers trembled over a protruding stomach hardened like stone.

Please, not now. I'm not ready. I'm not–

As she made her case to God, a more intense contraction interrupted her pleas. Overwhelming pain stole her vision and rolled her onto her side, crushing fresh sprouts reaching for new life in the summer sunlight. A welcome dampness permeated her dress and cooled her hot flesh. A ludicrous thought settled into her mind as the blinding pain prevented her next breath.

I've soiled the only sundress that fits me.

Fear-induced adrenaline flooded her bloodstream. A liquid rope of metallic saliva slid over her tongue and extended from her gaping mouth to kiss the soil beneath her shaking lips. She was moments from vomiting the little bile her stomach held when she gasped her first breath since trying to stand.

"Cora!" Mother's voice came sharply from the porch, draped in disappointment. "What on earth are you doing?"

With her lungs refilled, Cora tried to answer, but in her distress, she couldn't find her voice. Instead, a warm flow of relief coursed between her thighs and fed the garden.

Her water must have broken. Either that or she'd urinated on herself again. The former seemed more likely considering the excruciating pain overwhelming her body and how little she'd had to drink over the past two days. Every time she'd tried to drink water, she'd thrown it up. Mother insisted this was further evidence of God's disappointment with her daughter.

"He's showing you the error of your ways, little lamb. You're paying penance for opening yourself to that boy," Mother had said through gritted teeth as she grabbed a handful of Cora's hair and shook her head over the open toilet. Normally Cora would cry out in pain at such handling, but she'd grown numb to the abuse over the past few weeks. With every day her stomach presented more of the baby for the world to see, Mother grew more confident in her anger. Now, laying incapacitated on her side in the garden, Cora feared how Mother would react to her damaged sprouts.

"I'm … sorry," she managed.

Mother scrambled from the back porch and came to her like a brisk wind. Her rich chestnut curls danced about her shoulders as she went. She kneeled beside Cora, her vulnerable little lamb, and gently swept the loose dirt from her sun-kissed cheeks. Inspecting her lamb's lap, she ran her fingers through the tacky fluid coating her thighs. "Now, now, there's no time for apologies. We need to get you upstairs. It's about time for your rebirth."

Rebirth? What an odd word choice.

As Mother pulled on Cora's lanky, useless arms, the knotted muscles in her abdomen and legs untangled a notch. The medicine of Mother's touch had a way.

That's ridiculous. This isn't her work. You're simply falling into a lull between contractions, she thought.

"Stand, girl. On your feet." Mother's voice strained as she pulled harder on Cora's wrists. Cora planted her feet on the earth and pressed her body toward the spinning sky, unfolding as she came to her feet. Her wet dress separated from her skin as Mother shuffled her across the grass, up the porch steps, and to the rear of the house.

"Not here. Take me to town. To Doctor Blake," she pleaded between waves of nausea and static thoughts.

"You've lost your mind if you think I'm parading you into town like this. Putting your sin on display for the world to see. This happens here. I'll hear nothing more of Doctor Blake. Do you hear me?" Mother hurried their pace as they breached the back door and entered the dark, stale kitchenette. Spotless wood counters stretched around the room, interrupted only by the farm sink below the window and a wooden icebox in the far corner. The familiar smell of freshly spread pine oil met Cora's heightened senses. Her stomach squeezed hard against the scent.

Saliva flooded her mouth a moment before more bile rose to join it. Cora slammed her mouth shut. Mother saw.

"You'd better swallow it down, girl. Do *not* vomit on my floors, so help me God!"

Cora did as Mother commanded and exhaled a vile, hot breath as the fetid mix slid down her raw throat. A torrent of emotion welled up from somewhere desperate in her heart. Perhaps she was weak because of her youth, her inexperience. Perhaps the prospect of raising a child without a father overwhelmed her. And it wasn't Danny's fault. How could it be? He didn't know about Cora's pregnancy. Mother insisted on secrecy, said he wasn't fit to father a child, still a child himself, in fact. Mother insisted she'd be better off without him. Cora's heart ached to the contrary and had for her nearly seven months of awareness.

At night, when she quietly wept in the cool moonlight streaming through her window, she prayed he'd come to the house to inquire about her whereabouts. But Danny never came for her. She knew in the marrow of her bones Mother had gotten to him. She'd scared him away without disclosing their secret.

She'd never see him again if Mother had her way.

That seemed impossible in such a small town. Would she never bring her baby to town? Would she never return to school or see her friends again? Was that the price to pay for falling in love and bearing a child through that love? What once felt like a gift now felt like an impossible curse.

The baby's not a curse. God doesn't make mistakes.

Cora's tears came as they reached the stairs. She looked up beyond the steps and saw the open bathroom door to the left. Her bedroom door stood open to the right in the upstairs hall. Those doors looked a mile away. She tried to turn back toward the door, to return to the yard and her chores, to the dewy grass and the swaying trees.

"No, Cora. There's no getting out of this. Prepare your heart for God's work. Let's go." Mother pulled her back to the stairs. Cora sobbed and lifted one wet, shaking foot to the first stair, then the other. One foot, then the next, over and over. Reaching the top landing, she looked back and saw her wet footprints tracing her unsteady path up the stairs. Those footprints sang to her. Those footsteps felt like fate.

Cora leaned toward her bedroom and the sanctity of her bed, but Mother ushered her toward the bathroom.

"I want my bed," Cora cried. A flutter of butterflies with razor blade wings reinvigorated the pain in her abdomen.

"You'll ruin your bed, girl. We do this in the tub."

Mother reached into the shadows and flipped the bathroom light switch. The small, white-tiled room flashed to life. Bottomless dread replaced Cora's fear. This felt *terribly* wrong. She needed out *now*.

Cora turned to flee. Mother reached. Cora's feet slipped. Mother stood firm, her hands tightening like tourniquets around Cora's upper arms. The room sparkled in Cora's tears as Mother pulled her into the bathroom and shut the door.

Cora's body vibrated with a native instinctual energy as fear seized the helm of her mind. This energy blocked her eyes from seeing, her ears from hearing, her mind from recording memories. Through it all, one unexplainable detail emerged–the water filling the tub as they entered the room.

<hr>

"You've got to push, Cora. I know you're tired. But you're almost there."

They'd been at it for hours. Mother's order felt utterly impossible, yet inevitable. No matter how hard Cora pushed, her effort fell short. God, the *pressure* on her bowels scared her. Had she been sufficiently nourished, she'd fear spoiling the tub water. Even submerged in water, her pelvis felt heavy, burdened. However, she sensed an impending resolution ahead. She was so close to bringing life into the world. She'd been in the tub, legs braced on the porcelain walls, for what felt like an eternity. This had to end soon.

Mother stood and exhaled in frustration, stray hairs flitting in the air surrounding her frazzled head. Tub water soaked through her dress. Cora couldn't recall ever seeing Mother so disheveled.

"I'll be right back. Catch your breath." Mother darted from the room in a blur, leaving the door swinging from its hinges behind her.

Cool hall air flooded the room, raising bumps on Cora's exposed wet skin. A few seconds later, Mother returned with two freshly washed towels. She set one on the pedestal sink and brought the other to the tub.

"You're so close. Pull on this when I count to three."

Mother pushed the towel into Cora's trembling hands. She whimpered. Cora didn't want to pull on a towel. She wanted to climb out of this tub and hide from this room forever.

"Okay, here we go. One. Two. Three. Pull!"

Mother pulled. Daughter pulled.

As Cora bore down, her bottom *burned* as if doused with lit gasoline. Beneath the surface of the burning, Cora felt her baby's head expanding her flesh, displacing her natural structure. A moment later, she birthed her child's head, then its remaining slick, amniotic being followed. Cora collapsed as her baby left her, every muscle thrumming with adrenaline and an indescribable weariness. An immediate wave of ecstatic relief and exhaustion overcame her as she struggled to catch her breath.

Mother emerged from between her knees, holding a shiny gray body. Its arms and legs shook in quick pulses as Mother grabbed the towel from the sink and wiped it clean. Cora's vision blurred as she struggled to calm her breathing. The tingles in her extremities and static in her vision obscured her awareness. She wanted to hold her child.

"Is the baby okay? Why isn't it crying?"

Mother rubbed the baby vigorously, the muscles of her face wound tight as she looked the baby over. "She's trying. Come on, girl."

She's trying. Cora had a baby girl.

"Our ... girl ..." Cora's voice felt distant and dreamy. She tried to sit up but couldn't. Her stomach muscles refused to work. Cora slipped into unconsciousness as the room became a playground of shadows.

From unseen corners of the enveloping darkness, she heard her baby cry.

CHAPTER 7

MALLORY

Mallory panicked when Cora's baby entered their world without a terrified cry. She'd snatched the limp, gelatinous infant from the water and rolled her face up. Eyes closed, the small creature trembled in her hands, but it looked *wrong*. Mallory's eyes darted over the tiny gift.

A girl.

Why is her body so gray? Why isn't she moving or crying?

Over her years, Mallory had witnessed several deliveries, but there'd always been a doctor present, and she'd never seen a baby in such poor shape at birth.

She's not breathing.

Mallory's heart shifted a gear, her pulse racing. The umbilical cord was clear of the infant's neck, extending from child to mother. In the tub, Cora teetered on the edge of consciousness, likely unable to comprehend her mother's frantic response. She mumbled words Mallory couldn't make out as she rolled the baby face down on one arm and gave her several firm pats on the back before rolling her face up again. She searched the baby's face for a response.

Nothing.

"She's trying. Come on, girl..." She vigorously rubbed the newborn's tiny chest, willing its blood into action through her rough hands.

Check her mouth, she thought, feeling defeated by missing such a simple step. She pressed her pinky finger through the baby's open lips, her heart sinking into nostalgia as her finger found the baby's gums. Memories of rubbing Cora's gums when she was teething emerged bittersweet, beckoning tears to her eyes. But she had no time for sweet memories, her daughter needed her in more serious ways now than the past held. She was holding her baby's unresponsive child. What if she couldn't save her?

"Come on, little one." She scooped a mucus-rich liquid from the baby's mouth and wiped it on the hem of her house dress.

The frail creature resting on her right forearm gasped, lips quivering, face knotted. A shrill cry so beautiful it broke Mallory's panic ricocheted off the bathroom's hard surfaces.

Life. Here. In this moment.

Tears of relief coursed down Mallory's cheeks as she wiped the baby clean with a towel. Gray flesh turned to mottled pink as the tiny body flushed with oxygenated blood. Mallory finally had permission to reclaim her composure.

Not quite. Beyond the baby, she saw Cora slouching further into the tub, still unconscious, mouth inches from the water. Cora didn't appear well–*at all*. Slumped in the tub, eyes closed, her limp arms and legs twitched with misfiring nerves teetering on the edge of consciousness. A thick tendril of blood and afterbirth snaked from between her legs into the surrounding water alongside the taut umbilical cord.

If Mallory didn't help her soon, she may slip beneath the water and risk drowning. She needed to set the baby down and tend to *her* daughter, but she couldn't reach the floor beside the tub without severing baby from mother. Mallory remembered the knife she'd set in the sink for this very purpose.

First, help Cora.

Cradling the loosely wrapped baby with her left hand, Mallory pulled Cora up from the water by one limp arm.

"Damn it, Cora. I need you to wake up, baby. Come on, girl." Mallory's words slipped through lips pulled tight like steel cables as she hefted Cora's limp body into a seated position. With Cora momentarily safe, Mallory stretched past the tub to the sink and drew the knife from the basin.

Unexpectedly, time slowed as the knife settled into her palm like an old friend. The room grew quiet, the light less harsh, the threat of losing her daughter or the infant feeling less tangible.

Taking the knife felt like taking control. A foreign strength steadied her composure.

Cut.

Mallory knew that voice in her head like she knew her own. She tried to oppose, to reject the command but she couldn't. She had no voice, no fight in her. Only compliance. Mallory's breath calmed, her nerves no longer firing like a million synapses on a switchboard.

Cut.

"I—"

Cut.

"—won't."

You will.

The knife lowered, found its mark, and went to work. Mallory fought relentlessly to keep her eyes up, above the gory work. The sensation of warm fluid poured over her busy hand further convincing her to avoid *seeing*. Seeing was pointless anyways, her pilot had control. She didn't want to watch what she couldn't stop, what she couldn't control. Nausea washed through her. The thought of what she may be doing below her line of sight sickened her. Panicking in her shell, she tried to stop her arm from its hypnotic sawing motion but again, found she had no control. She blinked reflexively as a warm mist sprayed her face, coating her lips and cheeks. She fought the urge to lick the substance, to draw it in, to *taste*, and confirm what she suspected she was doing. But she would *never*. That *thing* that clung to her like a tumor would, but not her.

"Leave...us...alone." Mallory muttered through her mushy mouth as her knife finally broke through its fleshy prize.

Against her will, Mallory's head tipped downward, her eyes following the trajectory, forcing her to see what she'd done.

The umbilical cord lay in two parts. One end a bloody, exposed knot nestled on the newborn's belly and the other coiled over the edge of the tub resembling the world's thinnest roped sausage.

Never doubt me. Now bring her to me.

"I can't."

Mallory's faculties returned in a wave of misfiring nerves twitching muscles. She fled the bathroom for Cora's room and set the baby on a makeshift pallet of blankets on the floor. Mallory hated leaving the baby on the floor like that, but what choice did she have? She needed the bed for Cora and the last thing she wanted was the baby rolling off the bed in her absence.

You were a terrible mother to Cora, and now you're a terrible grandmother, too.

"Am not," she grumbled under her breath while flipping the covers back on the bed before darting back to the bathroom across the hall. Cora remained as she'd left her, unconscious in the tub. Mallory reached for the drain, hesitated, then committed her arm to the bloody, afterbirth infused bath water to pull the plug from the tub basin. The drain uttered a muffled gurgle as the soupy amalgamation slid through its mouth to the open pipes. The slurping, hungry sound turned Mallory's guts, but she kept her composure by concentrating on the task at hand.

She rinsed Cora, toweled her dry, and now had to carry her to the bedroom.

Although the girl was a slight thing, lifting and carrying her unconscious body was harder than Mallory expected. She barely reached the bed before her arms gave out against her will. Mallory spilled Cora onto the bed and manipulated her limbs under the retracted covers. Careful to protect the bedding from her daughter's weeping body,

Mallory placed several towels under and over Cora's hips before tucking her in. She stepped back and took in the room. Her daughter lay unconscious on the bed and the baby lay quietly on the pallet a few feet away. Mallory pressed two fingers to her daughter's neck and barely felt a pulse. Tears welled in Mallory's eyes as her fear threatened to surge.

What if Cora's bleeding increased through the night?

What if the girl woke in a panic when Mallory was elsewhere in the house? Would she try to leave the bed before realizing her circumstances?

What if she came looking for the baby?

Where would the baby sleep tonight?

When would she need her mother's milk?

What if Cora couldn't produce milk?

All these thoughts flooded Mallory's mind. She covered her face, choking back more tears. "I can't do this right now," she whimpered.

You're not alone. You just need a moment to think. Bring the baby to the sitting room.

Mallory did as her thoughts commanded.

CHAPTER 8

MALLORY

Seated in the silent sitting room downstairs, Mallory struggled to contain the emotions spurred by her new granddaughter resting in her exhausted arms. Swaddled and finally calmed from the trauma of birth, the baby girl whimpered between bouts of sleep. A dull ache settled into Mallory's chest. The baby resembled Cora at birth. Her swollen eyes and minuscule nose twitched with dream fodder. This experience was far more than Mallory had expected. Until that night, she'd convinced herself Cora should put the baby up for adoption, but now conflicting emotions fueled doubts. How could she acknowledge the child's striking resemblance to Cora and stand behind that proposition?

Because Cora's too young. If she keeps the baby, she'll be your responsibility, not hers.

Maybe that was the best-case scenario. What would she do if Cora didn't survive the night? She'd have no choice but to raise the child alone. She'd already been down that road once, and she couldn't fathom embarking on that journey again.

"That's not happening. She'll be fine." Tears welled in her eyes. Her heartache deepened with an anxious energy, the threads binding her control slowly unraveling.

"I can't do this right now. I just need to catch my breath," Mallory said, looking to the ceiling to constrain emerging tears. A cold, steady breath drifted from the fireplace's open mouth, cooling her exposed ankles. Mallory collected her emotions and surveyed the room. A narrow end table stood between two vacant wooden Shenandoah chairs, the impenetrable night pressing against the windows behind them. A portrait of Mallory and Cora sat prominently on the fireplace mantel.

Time stood still for Mallory once she gave her body over to the comfort of the sitting room couch. Her muscles burned and twitched as they relaxed, threatening to wake the nameless baby in her arms with each tremor.

A baby born out of wedlock, to a life without a father. Not that the young man had abandoned Cora, quite the contrary. Danny had tried to see her several times, but Mallory cut him off before he realized Cora was pregnant.

Mallory recognized utter heartbreak in him the day she cornered him outside Norge Market, his mother still roving the vegetable stands in search of suitable produce for the week. Mallory was blunt with him. Danny's brief love affair with her daughter, solely fueled by young lust, would have no time to flourish, no air to breathe. She forbade him from seeing her. She saw how her words bruised Danny's heart; he couldn't hide the truth from showing in the pained contours of his face. He loved Cora deeply.

Mallory also made sure no one else in town knew about the pregnancy, not even Dr. Blake. She'd taken Cora to a physician several hours west, near Amelia County, when she'd suspected Cora's condition. And she'd been right. A mother knows these things. But the town should not. They'd mark Cora as a whore, an unwed mother with weak morals and no future.

Mallory wouldn't let that happen.

She withdrew Cora from school the very next day and kept the girl at the house until she could figure out a long-term plan. After all, it made little sense to keep this nasty secret through the pregnancy and subsequently present the newborn in town. No, she would convince Cora to put the baby up for adoption. To date, that plan had failed miserably. Cora refused to consider any alternatives to motherhood.

And now here they were. Mother, baby, and all.

A numb eternity of thought passed in the dark sitting room before Mallory realized she and the baby weren't alone. The light dancing from the candelabra on the narrow end table cast shadows that played against each other on the walls surrounding Mallory and the baby. But the candles had nothing to do with how her own shadow ran in a silky river across the floor and gathered like black silt poured in a mold in the chair opposite her.

Shadow Mother spoke.

"You're exhausted."

Mallory sat as still as a statue but unsurprised by Mother's arrival. She was overdue for a visit. Shadow Mother had avoided her for weeks. Now, Mallory feared the purpose of her manifestation.

"I'll be fine once I get some rest." Mallory's heart pounded and she squirmed in her seat. A cool sweat broke over her forehead as her breathing deepened.

Shadow Mother shifted in her chair, thousands of tiny gleaming contours reflecting light like polished grains of black sand on a moonlit beach. Her words came from an immovable mouth.

"Be at ease, child. I see our girl has delivered."

Mallory pulled the bundle closer to her bosom. She felt pinned under the gaze of an attentive hunter. Shadow Mother continued.

"Now, now. There's no need to be anxious. There's no need for fear."

"Leave them alone," Mallory commanded, firm enough to stand her ground but low enough to not disturb the baby.

"Our Cora isn't doing too well upstairs, you know. She's lost quite a lot of blood. Too much," Shadow Mother said.

"She'll be fine. I'll nurse her back to health. I'm her mother." Mallory wasn't sure why she said that last sentence but it felt necessary.

"What a sweet confidence."

"I mean it. Stay away from her," Mallory insisted.

"You know you can't nurse her back, right? Not in time for Cora to feed that baby. How long do you think she'll last? She needs blood. Would you like to bleed for her?"

Mallory wasn't sure how to respond. She hardened her resistance through silence. In the space behind her eyes, she felt a loosening, a slip further into exhaustion.

"I'll bleed for..." Her sentence fell apart as her eyes grew heavy.

"Let me help. Give me the child in exchange for Cora. Let me solve all your problems."

Shadow Mother's words poured like hot caramel into Mallory's mind. A sweet confection to resolve her distress. For a moment, she thought the offer was too good to be true. No baby meant no hiding. Cora would have a new start.

Are you out of your mind? This is your grandbaby! And Cora would never approve of this. She's a mother, she'll go to the ends of the earth for her child, she thought.

Prying fingers breached Mallory's mind and pulled the thoughts from her gray matter. She felt utterly violated and defenseless.

"Settle down, Mallory. We've been together for too long. Aren't you sick of me? Present the child as an offering to me and I'll restore Cora's health and leave you for good."

Mallory's mind spun. This Shadow Mother, this darkness, had clung to her for as long as she could remember. A demon initially confused for unjustified jealousy, bottomless depression, and unbridled hatred, Shadow Mother was as real to her as the sun. As inevitable as death. Her dark angel.

"I don't believe you. You...you love me." Mallory struggled to keep her words intact. A drunken perspective settled into her vision.

"I *do* love you. That's why I want to do this for you. Let me save your daughter. You'll never forgive yourself if you don't."

Mallory leveraged silence.

"You'll kill her if you refuse me," Shadow Mother hissed.

"She'd never forgive me for giving up her child," Mallory slurred.

"Forgiveness is a luxury of the living," Shadow Mother replied.

Mallory's arms dropped an inch, then another. Her grip loosened. The baby stirred. She must be hungry by now. Perhaps starving. Mallory couldn't care for this baby without Cora. She wouldn't.

Her arms dropped lower, now to her lap.

"No. She...I...can't."

"Ah, I know how to make this better. You keep the baby and I'll go to Cora while you lay here incapacitated. I'll leave you alone for the first time in your pathetic life and attach myself to *your* baby. What a treat! She'll feel the pain you've felt all these years as she slips into death. She'll have this endless despair, this crushing depression, as her final emotion. Rather than longing for your love, she'll drown in resentment, feeling abandoned and utterly hopeless. Your ultimate gift to your child." Shadow Mother's voice wavered, gritty and vile. "You know, children normally call out for their mothers when they die. I'll see to it she curses you with her last breath."

Smothered in fear, held captive by Shadow Mother's demonic possession, Mallory screamed without a sound. Her mouth hung open but only a pathetic *pleeeeeeeeeee* escaped her throat.

"Yes, that's it," Shadow Mother said, holding her arms out as she leaned forward in her chair. "Consider your sweet Cora."

Mallory's arms went limp, and the baby teetered, rolled down her belly into her lap, then tumbled to the floor.

Shadow Mother drained from her chair like a snake fleeing a bush as Mallory's head snapped back, casting her vision to the ceiling. Somewhere on the floor around her feet, the baby screamed out. Dropped to the floor, the baby cried for her mother, her grandmother, for anyone.

the baby the baby the baby the baby

Mallory's mind skipped like a stone across an endless expanse of terror. Slowly, Shadow Mother emerged in her vision, morphing into a smoky black presence a foot above her upturned face.

"Say yes. Say you'll save Cora."

Black tendrils dipped down and tickled Mallory's quivering lips, coaxing her words forth.

"Save. My. Baby."

Smiling, Shadow Mother poured down into Mallory's open eyes. Blind and terrified, Mallory went rigid and gave herself over to Shadow Mother as she had so many other times. But tonight's violation came with new consequences. A life for a life. And although the baby had stopped screaming beyond the charcoal cloud enveloping Mallory, her shrill cries echoed in the vast wasteland of Mallory's broken mind. Then silence.

It was done.

CHAPTER 9

CORA

ora pushed but the baby refused to emerge from her. She wasn't sure how long she'd been in labor but it felt like an eternity. Her mother darted from the room and back, returning each time carrying something different.

A stack of towels.

A bottle of clear liquid, likely pure alcohol.

A tray containing sewing needles and thread.

Another bottle, this one yellowed from the hydrogen per-oxide inside.

She's not planning to sew me up, is she? *she thought.*

Cora tried to sit up taller in the tub, but an overwhelming contraction kept her in place. She tried breathing through the pain but couldn't draw air. Her lungs refused to comply.

Mother left again.

Cora's eyes shot to the murky water between her spread thighs. Doubt bloomed in her mind. Perhaps a water birth was a terrible idea. What if the baby came out while Mother scavenged the house for supplies? Would she have the strength to snatch the baby from the water and keep it from drowning? She'd have to. What option did she have?

Mother returned. She carried a hammer and several boards cut the length of the tub. She dropped the boards to the floor beside the tub, exhaled while stretching her arms above her head.

"What are you doing? Why did you bring those?" Cora asked through clenched teeth.

"I have a lot of work to do, dear. Someone must clean up your mess." Mother held a closed hand out in front of her, palm down. She opened her fingers and a dozen steel nails rained from her palm. Each nail screamed on contact with the tiled floor, grating punctuations blistering Cora's ears.

A crippling contraction shot through Cora's gut, seizing her body and driving the air from her lungs.

The baby emerged. A sulfuric cloud of black afterbirth flowed from Cora, turning the tub water to liquid graphite. Mother snatched the child from the water, its umbilical cord still attached to her pulsing womb. Water poured from the squirming child. A big breath. A piercing cry.

Mother placed the baby on the floor. Gripping the sides of the tub, Cora pulled her body up. As her eyes broke over the tub's lip, she saw Mother place the baby amongst the boards on the floor. She lifted one board and nailed it to another as the baby screeched and writhed on the wet tile.

Cora screamed. "Give me my baby!"

"Don't worry, dear. You're going with her." Mother smiled and raised the hammer.

Cora reached for her but something grabbed her head, pulling her back from the tub's edge. Two black hands reached from beneath the tub's sloshing liquid, clawing and pulling. One grabbed a handful of her hair, the other covered her mouth.

Down she went, the black liquid stealing Cora from the bathroom.

Cora opened her eyes to a new darkness. She tried to sit up but couldn't. Her hands scrambled to remove the water-borne assailant pulling her under. But they found nothing. She was alone in the night, dreaming in bed.

No hands.

No tub.

No water.

Cora exhaled in relief, her hands instinctively going to her belly. Her breath caught in her throat again. Her stomach was smaller, softer—changed.

The baby.

Alarms chimed in her head.

"Be easy, Cora. You're okay." Mother stood in the open doorway to her left, holding something small in her hands. Cora could barely see her face in the deep shadows.

"What's happening? Where is my baby?" The question sounded strange falling from her slurring mouth. Even after nine months of pregnancy, she struggled to acknowledge she had a child now.

"Don't worry about her. You need to rest. You lost a lot of blood." Mother crossed the dark room and sat on the bed beside her. "Drink this."

A teacup chattered against a saucer in Mother's hands. She stirred the cup's contents, then placed the spoon on the nightstand. Normally, Mother would fuss mightily if Cora placed a wet spoon directly on the wood surface, but tonight she seemed not to care.

"Here. Drink deeply." Mother pressed the porcelain cup to her mouth.

The fragrant tea smelled earthy and bright. Its steam kissed her lips, leaving a dampness for her mouth to crave.

Cora drank the tea in several big swallows as Mother instructed. A comforting warmth spread through her exhausted body. Her pounding headache quieted, her sore stomach muscles numbed, and her weary body relaxed into the mattress and pillows. Her arms felt unusually heavy, like she wore chain mail, her muscles weak and useless against gravity. Mother was right; she needed rest.

"The tea is wonderful," Cora muttered, her mouth struggling to form the words as her eyelids met. Her tongue pressed to the roof of her mouth like a swollen wad of cotton filling her mouth. As she melted into her pillow, she fell closer to the edge of a dream, toward a limitless landscape of darkness streaked with vibrant rivers of melding colors.

Thus began the unraveling of Cora's reality.

CHAPTER 10

MALLORY

Mallory sat catatonic in the dead silence of the witching hour. Most days, the backyard served as her busy place, her garden demanding her love and returning it in spades. However, most nights, cloaked in moonlight and glowing cloud cover, it served as her sanctuary—a dark reprieve from the energy within the house.

She couldn't recall a time when she had needed that reprieve more than on this night. Everything was falling apart. Cora slept in her bed, drugged and traumatized from giving birth. And somewhere unknown to Mallory, Shadow Mother had the baby. A nameless bastard child born from sin, but Cora's child, nonetheless.

What could Mallory do? Her life felt like an unrelenting sequence of tragedies.

Since her youth, Mallory had sensed her home turn sour with the sun's descent, when the shadows emerged from waiting corners and devious angles of inanimate objects thrummed with Shadow Mother's spirit. It had been this way all these years, and likely would remain so.

Light and dark and the interface between them.

Frankly, she knew no different. Mallory lived each day on the treacherous precipice of a home inhabited by a spiritual energy she could never harness but would always know in intimate ways. Often, she likened her existence to that of a woman married to a man with an unpredictable nature. When her spouse loved her, the love sang an unmatched tune, filling her heart with unrivaled bliss. But when her spouse deceived her, the bond turned bitter and ugly.

Such was love, she supposed. Such was her existence, albeit riddled with tragedy from the days of her earliest memories.

Of all the relationships Mallory had lost, her mother's impacted her most. Mother had loved her dearly, more than Mallory could ever love Cora, she feared. Heaven knew she'd tried to match her mother's love, but she'd never felt the same intensity for another human that she found in her mother's eyes.

In some ways, Mallory believed their love had been too much for her mother to bear. It may have crushed her under its weight. Mother had suffered from adult-onset schizophrenia, committed to Eastern State Psychiatric Hospital when Mallory was eight years old. Months later, Mother died there, removed from the child she loved more than life.

Shadow Mother arrived shortly afterward.

All these years later, Mallory believed she'd manifested Shadow Mother in her young desperation.

At first, she'd experienced moments of comfort and whimsy so gentle, they convinced her Mother was with her in spirit. She'd close her eyes and smell Mother's hair cascading over her face. Then, more intense physical sensations came. Mother cradled her in bed at night, lacing her forehead with kisses. Mother's whispers filled her upturned ear as she lay mid-dream in the wide, solid band of moonlight penetrating her bedroom window.

"I love you, Mallory."

Some nights it was, "Mommy's here."

Other nights, "I love you forever, little lamb."

The night became a wonderland of love, a stark contrast from her days of silent mourning in the shadow of her father's broken heart. Father did his best to raise her despite his emotional wounds. He kept a brave face, but his efforts weakened as the days wound on. Some nights, she'd hear Father speaking to someone in his room. Was he speaking to her mother's spirit? Perhaps he had his own Shadow Mother. Mallory tried to ask once, but he became visibly upset and ended the conversation by simply saying, "Your mother is dead. We need to move on."

Despite his passionate advice, he never did. He honored her mother by loving Mallory as best he could, but the man's heart never recovered. She was never enough.

Mother's passing had been the first domino to fall, and the second was Mallory's marriage. She'd given herself to Joseph in a rushed marriage only a year before she had Cora. Father accepted the marriage, although he wasn't very fond of Joseph. Said something about the man rubbed him the wrong way. But Father supported her because Mallory asked him to.

Mallory and Cora barely survived childbirth. She'd heard complicated pregnancies normally created an unbreakable bond between a mother and child, but Mallory struggled to love Cora as Mother had loved her. In fact, she never loved another person as deeply. Not Joseph, not Father, and sadly, not Cora. For many years, Mallory believed Shadow Mother could fill that void. But the years took their toll on those around her, proving her terribly wrong. The love waned with every loss. Inevitably, the second domino fell.

A month after Cora's birth, Joseph died in an accident at the lumberyard in West Point. A mountain of logs collapsed on him, crushing him to death. A quick but incomprehensibly brutal death. No one deserved to die like that, especially Joseph.

Then, only three months after Mallory buried her young husband, her father died in his sleep.

Life had a cruel way with her. Mallory wondered if death would treat her more fairly. She wished to join Mother, Father, and Joseph but she had to live for Cora.

Oh, she'd had opportunities to join them. Every moment alone in the house while baby Cora napped in her room became an opportunity to dwell on death, on the loss she'd experienced, on what waited for her on the other side. And Shadow Mother did her best to keep Mallory trapped in those thoughts, tempting her but never pushing hard enough to exact action. Maybe one day she'd finally give in but not until Cora grew up and became her own woman. Raising her child was Mallory's only remaining opportunity to honor her mother's love. It was her duty. And she found moments of joy embedded among the pain. Afternoons chasing butterflies with Cora in the backyard, candlelit nights together in the sitting room reading Aesop's fables and Charles Dickens novels—they had their joy. But alone, at night when she faced the terminal darkness of grief and Shadow Mother returned to her dreams, Mallory experienced her pain in spades.

She never sought a social life, choosing isolation with Cora and the ghosts of her dead loved ones over reconnecting with childhood friends or seeking another marriage. Of course, the isolation came with risks. If she succumbed to her suicidal urges or became terminally ill, she'd leave Cora to strangers. Mallory had cousins in neighboring towns but none close enough to trust with Cora. Shadow Mother offered to relieve Mallory of her grief and to love Cora for an eternity. But Mallory feared what that meant for Cora.

Mallory knew Shadow Mother was real, but how could she describe her to any sane adult without being committed to an institution like her mother? Besides, she had no answers to the questions that would inevitably follow. She wasn't sure why Shadow Mother existed or where she'd come from. Was she a product of Mallory's traumatized mind? Or did she suffer from schizophrenia like her mother?

No one knew the answers to those questions, especially not Mallory.

Now, she found herself at an impasse. Should she pursue Shadow Mother and fight for Cora's child?

In many ways, Shadow Mother had relieved Cora of her burden, from the life of an unwed mother in a society lacking an appetite for such an arrangement.

I don't care about this town and its narrow minds. She could live here with me.

Mallory knew that was a pipe dream. Cora wanted more from life. Much more. She wanted all the things Mallory had lost or given up on: a husband, a house full of children, a life.

That life could have started with this baby.

What have I done? How could I have let her take the baby?

A familiar darkness replied. *You've betrayed your daughter, the one person in the world who depends on you most. You don't deserve her, but I let you have her. Don't forget our deal. What's done is done. Now clean up your mess and honor your word.*

Mallory's skin boiled and tried to slide from her bones. She was livid, yet terrified. Shadow Mother was right; she'd spent her night leveraging her broken past to justify backing out of the deal.

What's done is done. There's no turning back. Love your daughter while you can. You're lucky I'm not taking her to teach you a lesson.

Dread and regret intertwined in her anxious chest, an ugly knot forming where her heart pounded. Suddenly, the idea of leaving Cora alone upstairs after the night they'd had seemed extremely negligent. She should have stayed with her.

And you drugged her. What kind of mother does that? And how long do you think you can keep her drugged and unaware? Eventually, you'll have to tell her what you've done. Eventually, she'll know what you really are—a destroyer of people. Do I need to rescue her from you? Should I take her, too?

"You leave Cora alone!" Mallory snapped, coming abruptly to her feet to face the towering house. Cool moonlight lent the house's white siding an ethereal glow.

Shadow Mother stood prominently in Mallory's bedroom window, her substance a roiling black ectoplasm, a swaddled bundle in her arms.

You tend to your child and I'll tend to mine. Shadow Mother's voice uncoiled in Mallory's mind like a poisonous viper preparing to strike.

Once again, Mallory abandoned the moonlit yard for the perils of her home.

CHAPTER II
CORA

Like a balloon in a hurricane, Cora bobbed violently in the static between vivid, horrid dreams and a disorienting fog of awareness. She tried to plant her feet, to drop her mind to an acceptable altitude, but the ground never seemed close enough for her feet to find purchase.

Then darkness. Mumbling numbness. Another deep swallow and another flight from reality. An endless cycle unraveled with her caught in the whirlpool of semiconsciousness, a jostling helix spiraling downward without end.

In the moist, inescapable cavern at the bottom of the helix, the darkness deepened to inconceivable density, countered only by the maddening cries of a terrified and manic infant. Cora couldn't bear another second of the child's agony. She came apart, the infant's voice slicing her in two from crown to heel. Her body fell into coequal slabs of quivering viscera. Then, quartered, diced, minced by the compounding cries, blistering in their intensity. That's where Mother resided, in an abyss of shadow so impenetrable her mind ceased to function. Cora's life narrowed to a pinpoint, a concentrated mass of finite energy, then rebounded back to infinite spirit, expanding into form, returned to the mold, freed from its binding.

Cora couldn't orient herself in it all. She prayed for the ride to stop, for the conductor to pull the brake and let her off.

But that moment never came.

Light returned, mottled by the multicolored shade of her closed eyelids. She'd give anything to open them. But that felt inexplicably dangerous. Instead, she played it safe, choosing the shelter of shadow over the danger of exposure.

Is that sunlight trying to reach me from the other side?

But there was only one side, wasn't there? Even without vision, she knew which side she was on. She was on the outside, on an open, uninterrupted plain, land, sea, and air stretching out in all directions but impossible to see in detail.

Why wasn't she at home? In bed? Was she *ever* in bed? Maybe she'd always been here in the great expanse, and the concept of rest, of *home*, was nothing more than a degradation of her productive mind. Always dark, never understood, the vast plain was good enough for her. It had to be. It's all she had.

CHAPTER 12

MALLORY

Ten sleepless nights after Cora's delivery, Mallory crept into her daughter's room. The last morphine-infused teacup chattered on the delicate china saucer in her hand. The exceptionally strong morphine doses she'd fed Cora for over a week far exceeded any rational prescription, and she'd reached the end of her supply.

Nervous tremors idled Mallory's hands. The time had come to confront her daughter about their new reality. She wasn't ready to confess her sins to Cora—to lie *again*. She needed more time to prepare a suitable defense. The deal she'd struck with Shadow Mother was an unspeakable compromise to salvage Cora's future—a brutal demonstration of a mother protecting her child. But Mallory couldn't share this truth; she'd never told Cora about her lifelong struggle to coexist with Shadow Mother. Without context, how could Cora understand her mother's sacrifice? She'd be furious, confused, inconsolable. No story would suffice when the price for her mother's peace came at the unbearable cost of *her* child, *her* motherhood.

A daughter for a daughter. A trade so terribly unequal in its costs. A childhood, youthful beauty, innocence, and unending love, exchanged for the life of a young adult with no foreseeable path to love. A persistent sense of dread, the crushing ocean of regret she'd wallowed in since Shadow Mother had dealt her this hand, overcame Mallory. Coming through this, Cora would despise, not love, her mother.

Cora had no one left to love. No father. No grandparents. No lover. No child.

"She has me," Mallory pleaded, her mouth twisting to contain a sob. She'd never overcome this mistake, this curse.

This murder. And it was murder, wasn't it? While she didn't know what Shadow Mother had done with the infant, she knew the child was gone.

Murder.

You don't know that! And Cora would do the same if she were in my position, Mallory thought as she set the drink on the bedside table beside a soiled handkerchief and a flameless candelabra. The light contact of the saucer meeting the hard wood sounded like a thunderclap in the deafening silence of the home. Her throat tightened as she fought back an ascending surge of emotion.

"She would have done the same," she repeated aloud. Cryptically, Cora's sedated head shook in a faint, restricted arc on her soiled pillow. Mallory leaned in to make sure Cora remained suspended well below the surface of consciousness. The girl's fluttering eyes and deep, drawn breaths convinced Mallory.

But was that true? Would Cora have made the same deal? She'd yet to meet, let alone *know,* her child. She hadn't seen the child beyond the bulge in her belly, beyond the dream of what motherhood may bring. How could she possibly think her own life was less valuable than that of a total stranger?

The child is nothing but a dream to Cora.

On cue, a pathetic whimper seeped from Cora's partially slack mouth. The desperate sound pulled Mallory's tears closer to the surface, a response to her motherly instinct to protect Cora from whatever chased her in that drug-induced dreamscape. Mallory leaned closer and whispered into Cora's unaware face.

"Nothing but a dream."

A familiar voice clamored into her ears and pierced her thoughts. Shadow Mother spoke, her voice like poison. *"Nothing but a dream."*

"Nothing but a dream," Mallory repeated. Her shadow peeled from her exposed skin, a thin filament of darkness suspended in the air between her and Cora.

"Nothing but a dream."

Mallory stumbled and caught herself from falling onto Cora laying in the bed. The shadow thickened, pouring from her loosely hanging hair into her face, extending from her shaking arms into mirror limbs. Assembling, co-agulating. Becoming.

"Nothing but a dream."

"No…" Mallory cut the repetition short, fought to change the script, to regain control over the demon filling the space between her and her helpless daughter on the bed.

Shadow Mother fully materialized, now inches from her face. Her density, manifesting in a roiling smoke, stung Mallory's nose, tendrils penetrating her sinuses and reaching Mallory's brain. Her vision blurred momentarily, then left her blind and helpless.

"No," she tried again. This time, her defiance brought crippling pain from the back of her throat to the base of her lungs.

Shadow Mother filled her until her ballooning lungs threatened to burst. The urge to cry out overwhelmed Mallory. Her lips closed in the column of shadow violating her mouth, trying to form words around her offender.

"No...nothing...nothing but a dream." Mallory's tears poured down her face like twin acid veins cutting arroyos in the tender flesh of her cheeks.

"Good girl." Shadow Mother's voice rang like a tuning fork in Mallory's ears, resonating through her mind, wiping her thoughts. She tried to shake her head, to deny confirmation of compliance, but she'd lost command of her motor skills. She'd lost herself to the demon in a way she'd never experienced before. This was fresh punishment.

Without a mouth to speak, she tried to think her opposition.

You've done this to us. You're the terrible mother, not me. I wish you'd never found me. I want my mother back. I–

An unseen hand snapped Mallory's head downward with such violence she momentarily feared her neck had broken, the upper vertebrae of her spine trying to breach the skin on the back of her neck. Her vision returned in a flash. She frantically blinked tears from her eyes so she could see.

Two raging eyes born of hellfire hovered inches from her own in the dense sulfuric abomination before her. Shadow

Mother slithered backward onto the bed, mounting Cora like a hunter pinning her prey before bringing a death blow. Shadow Mother's mouth opened, her rotting gray tongue uncoiling like a tentacle between her blackened teeth.

"I'll take her instead if you'd like, you ungrateful bitch. I'll take them both. Deal be damned." She leaned into Cora's face, tongue dancing over Cora's lips. "I'll breathe my death into her, take her against her will, press harder when she resists, choke the life from her panicked body while you watch. But that'll just be the start for us. I'll inhabit her; we'll spend the rest of our lives together. I'll wear her corpse for you, a crudely animated gift, her eyes filled with my energy. You'll feel my death through her frigid skin when we embrace. You'll beg me to take you instead, but I'll spare you and I'll wait years for your inevitable demise, for your god to claim you. As you near death and its sweet relief from our hell together, I'll drop her body at your feet, your last sight on the earth, then steal you for myself and drown you in the flow for eternity. Keep you from reuniting with your earthly mother, suspend you from ever seeing Cora as you once did."

Mallory's body quaked with fear, her nerves a misfiring rat's nest. The wrong move felt imminent, dangerous words dancing on her tongue. One poor response and she'd lose Cora to this demon. A disorienting sense of permanence prevailed, this curse enduring beyond them, reaching into generations, into a time outside her, into her bloodline.

"Please don't. Take me if you must."

Shadow Mother's tongue retracted as she sat erect and turned to Mallory. "Face your daughter. Tell her what you've done. Break her heart. Destroy her love for you. Give me my prize."

"The infant was your prize. We had a deal."

She was in a dance with the devil. She realized that she'd underestimated their terms of agreement. Mallory had given up much more than the baby. She'd given *them* up as well.

She wants to watch us suffer. That's what brings her joy, Mallory thought. A grin spread across Shadow Mother's smoky form in confirmation.

Cora stirred, her limbs twitching and her voice fighting to surface in her throat again.

"The morphine is wearing thin. Send her under one last time, then face your new reality, Mallory." Shadow Mother's form pulled tighter, then slithered from the bed, across the dusty floor, and climbed up Mallory's unsteady legs. Shadow Mother's voice returned to Mallory's head as the coal cloud consumed her features.

Nothing but a dream.

Shadow Mother retreated into Mallory's edges as she collapsed onto Cora's moaning body. She dug her fingers into her daughter's overheating body, desperate to show her how much she loved her, how she'd do anything to reverse this, to take her from this place forever and start over. But she couldn't. Shadow Mother wasn't in this home. She was in *them*.

"I love you, Cora," Mallory sobbed. She buried her face in her daughter's heaving chest, pulling her hard into her unworthiness. "I won't let her have you, even if you hate me for it."

Shadow Mother persisted. *Nothing but a dream. Say it, or else...*

Cora's heartbeat thrummed through her gown and bedsheets into Mallory's sobbing face.

Mallory did as she was told.

"Nothing but a dream."

CHAPTER 13

CORA

A weightlessness, like being suspended in deep water, held Cora's body in midair above her bed. She recalled descending, hovering close to her lumpy, inconsistent mattress several times recently, but she'd failed to make contact. Mother had visited, fed her, then sent her back toward the ceiling like one of those hot air balloons she'd learned about in school. How long had she been in this soupy atmosphere, cradled by invisible hands, suspended from wire above a firm reality?

The echo of footsteps climbing the stairs and reaching the landing outside her bedroom door interrupted her thoughts. A barely audible knock preceded her mother's entrance to the room. Cora craned her neck to see her mother's concerned face, her eyes red from crying and cheeks sagging with worry. Mother stared at the mattress below her. She was probably upset with Cora's disobedi-ence—she'd been ordered to stay in bed.

Mother carried another cup, likely containing more tea. No food this time, apparently.

When did she last eat?

Truthfully, she wasn't hungry. She just wanted to get to work. She had so much to do. Mother's garden required her studious eye, strong young hands, and capable back. So much neglected work—

"She has me," Mother said, looking down at the empty bed as if Cora lay beneath the sheets.

Who is she talking about? Who is she talking *to*?

This happened often...Mother talking to herself. Cora worried about Mother's loneliness getting the best of her. Without Cora, she had no other friends or family in her life. She'd lost most and shunned the others.

"Nothing but a dream," Mother spoke in a distant voice. Her lips trembled with emotion.

Am I dreaming? No, this was too real to be a dream. Cora had slept through the night and risen with the sun like she always does. Except she'd awoken in this precarious state, and, for some odd reason, she was quite happy about it.

Mother reached up and pulled her closer by an invisible thread.

"Oh, thank you, Mother. All this floating is getting to me. Don't get me wrong, I enjoy defying gravity, although I'm unsure how it's possible. Most of what I've experienced since our last trip to the garden feels impossible. More importantly, I'm ready to see my baby girl. Is she well? We owe her a name, you know."

Yes, a name. She'd considered many since the girl's birth, which seemed light years behind her now. She'd settled on Clara. Cora wasn't sure where she'd first heard it, but it fit. Of course, she hadn't discussed names with Mother yet, and she was sure Mother probably had a name firmly decided upon, some family name Cora had never heard or cared much to learn. Life felt surreal. Just a few days ago, she'd been unconcerned with family lineage or history. It seemed incredibly important now...but why?

Somewhere far from this room, on the other side of the house, baby Clara's voice pressed through wood and plaster. She's here. A link in the chain, a new page in our book, her contribution to this world that seemed oblivious to her.

"I hear you! Mommy hears you, little one. Mother, help me. I need to see her."

"Nothing but a dream." Mother kept repeating. She seemed fixated on her thoughts above the surrounding reality. This was nothing new. Cora often found her whispering phrases at the kitchen counter or in the sitting room. Those moments unsettled Cora and caused her great concern. But what could she do to stop them besides get Mother's attention? Usually, Mother came out of it easily, but today she looked weary and serious, her features drawn and thin in a way Cora had never seen.

"If I'm too unwell to walk, bring her to me. I must see her, Mother."

With one hand on Cora's left shin and the other on her chest, Mother pulled her closer to the bed and pressed her into the mattress. Cora's heart beat harder now that she'd heard her child's voice again. She'd been so forgetful, so absentminded, and neglected the girl. Mother had things under control, cared for the baby in Cora's absence. She'd told Cora the child's birth had nearly killed her. The medicine would have her right as rain soon...

The medicine. The teacup. She yearned for more, her bones craving the elixir, the warm, settling wave of comfort it provided. Somehow, she suspected her healing was her baby's healing as well. A mutual benefit communicated from mother to child. She didn't know how that worked but it didn't matter if she did. She simply understood it to be true. Like when the moon passed through its cycles and the tides responded in kind.

"Nothing but a dream." Mother's distant voice pulled Cora's thoughts back to the room.

Mother placed a knee on the mattress. A hand. Another knee.

Is she climbing into bed with me?

Cora struggled to clear her mind and focus her vision but failed. The medicine held her faculties and skewed her vision. Her eyelids remained immovable and the room darkened as a shadow interfered with the fuzzy scenery.

Weight, tangible and suffocating, pressed into her gut, her legs, her wrists. Her vision blackened, then returned clearer. Mother was sitting on her thighs, shimmying up to her torso and back again, skittish and—smiling?

Cora tried to lift her hands but Mother held them firm, leaning into them with her adult weight. Cora suddenly felt smaller, less powerful.

"Mother, no. What are you doing?" Cora thought she felt pain in her wrists but, no, she simply felt *intense* pressure. Immense, debilitating pressure.

The smell of freshly turned soil wafted from Mother, her hands hot and slick with sweat. Cora saw her face glistening in the fuzz, lacking detail but exhibiting shine. Her eyes seemed to glow in the obscure details.

Mother pressed her face to hers. Her wet tongue slipped from her mouth and probed Cora's lips.

Cora nearly screamed. But she lacked a voice, a physical response, or any sense of agency. The scent of roses and turned Virginia clay slipped from Mother's mouth to Cora's nose.

Cora last smelled that clay in the garden but roses *and* clay? A funeral. The image of a freshly dug grave in the family cemetery came together in her mind, a thousand disparate images cascading into a pile, then flattening into a discernible image. A shovel stood erect in the dirt beside the grave, a starling perched on the handle.

"Hello, Cora."

Not Mother...but *Mother*. Cora blinked hard and fast, her sight revealing a dreamlike distortion of Mother, her skin pitch black and glittering with mineral shine, radiant eyes like burning coals from the sitting room fireplace in winter. The woman's rich curls spilled about her shoulders to tickle Cora's face. Mysteriously, Cora didn't feel them, but she felt Mother's warm saliva drying on her parched lips. Locks of Mother's hair floated in the air about her face, held captive by the thick atmosphere. Cora wondered if they'd float from the bed together soon.

"That baby of yours is so...beautiful." Thick black tears filled Mother's eyes. "But you can't have her. She's mine."

"What are you talking about?" Cora asked. Mother's onyx form blacked out the room's natural light, drawing the space close to complete darkness. While Cora couldn't see beyond Mother, she sensed someone else in the room with them, standing over them, beside them. Cora's heart pounded, but she couldn't feel her veins pulsing. She was completely numb now.

"Your mother isn't what you think, girl. She's broken. She's incapable of love. You know this."

Cora tried to understand but struggled to make sense of Mother's words. Mother continued.

"When you wake, your body punished from a lack of movement, you'll search for your child. But you won't find her. You'll seek answers from your mother, and she'll lie to you to cover her sins. Remember, this is her fault. She's your enemy."

"Don't you hurt my baby," Cora mumbled. She felt Mother's moist tongue on her lips again and tried to pull away but couldn't.

"Drink, Cora. You *must* drink." Mother's voice, different now, lighter, softer, pleaded with her from somewhere else entirely.

Cora's body felt light again. She drifted up into the darkness, the clouds as dark as graphite parting to reveal a million stars assembling ahead.

I've ascended to the night sky, she thought wistfully. The vast expanse of space consumed her like stardust. Mother's voice, barely audible now, reached her across the expanding chasm between realities.

"Nothing but a dream."

CHAPTER 14

MALLORY

Mallory sobbed uncontrollably in the unlit hallway outside Cora's closed door. The confrontation with Shadow Mother over Cora's healing body had decimated her gnarled nerves. Things had spiraled out of control. Shadow Mother had become more aggressive, more evil than Mallory could have predicted. She had to get control of their situation and regain Cora's trust. Despite the girl's recent behavior and problematic circumstances, Cora was her life, the one person left in this world for Mallory to love and nurture. The prospect of losing her over Shadow Mother's deception felt imminent, unacceptable, unbearable. She couldn't let it happen. She'd make this right, pilot them through this perilous shoal water. They'd heal with time. If they were together, they had a chance at happiness.

Intent on devising a plan while she worked, Mallory wiped her tears, turned from Cora's bedroom door, and descended the stairs in a determined gallop.

She'd find her answers in her garden.

Her harvest awaited.

Late afternoon sunlight illuminated the hope remaining in Mallory's troubled heart. Although her knees ached and her back felt on the verge of a spasm, she worked without concern for her aging body, thinking only about how to make things right with Cora.

Her hands moved between earthbound potatoes while she silently reprimanded herself for not seeking answers through her faith, in meaningful prayer and supplication. She was a devout woman, but like most, she found belief easiest when life went well, and prayer easiest when life went poorly. Such was the trap of human nature, the dichotomy of comfort and distress. A new energy filled her soul as she spoke to God with her heart and worked the spuds with her hands.

Lord, bring us your salvation. Grant us your wisdom to endure this trial. And deliver us from the evil haunting us. Protect us, dear Father–

Mallory held her breath as she extracted a stubborn spud from the soil. She inspected the potato's skin for damage and smiled when she found none, placing the keeper in her basket like a freshly caught fish.

I'll do anything to keep her, Father. Anything. I've never questioned your will, especially your decision to take my mother from me so early in life or my husband so early in our marriage. My spirit broke, but I looked past the pain and sought your love in the heartache. Let me have love this time. Give me Cora. She needs–

Mallory froze, her hand on a strange body beneath the garden. Her eyebrows drew tight as she slowly drew her right hand from the soil.

Flesh breached the surface, the supple, tender foot of an infant. The lower leg extended beneath the soil, the rest of the tiny body set to the earth like an anchor. Mallory's fingers squeezed tight, then shot open, releasing the leg to the garden like a viper drawn from the earth. She screamed and scrambled backward, feet kicking and slipping in the loose dirt and slick grass bordering the garden.

"My God!"

The cloudless sky bobbed and arced above her as she clambered to her feet, desperate to run, to flee the garden and put distance between her and her macabre discovery.

Why panic? This is your work. Shadow Mother's voice broke through the chaos of her mind.

Mallory stumbled, then spun on her heels to face the house, her right hand held far from her body as if covered in disease. Her eyes darted from window to window but found them empty.

"Leave us alone!" Her voice broke as she screamed at the house.

"Your work," Shadow Mother replied.

Visions blitzed Mallory's mind, replacing her physical vision with unspeakable imagery.

Mallory, walking from the house, a newborn swaddled in her arms.

The pregnant moon consuming the night sky.

Dropping to her knees in the grass.

Hands digging, pulling, deeper.

Tears streaming.

The baby held up to the moon.

Baby pressed into the earth.

Swaddled in organic matter.

Shadows dancing in the leaves and stalks.

Mother dancing with the moonlight.

Sprinting down the cemetery path.

Trees whipping by, fencing the living from the dead.

Shadow Mother running alongside.

Shadow spirits flitting through the forest, yelping and feral.

Mother screaming.

Bloody throat.

Graves breached.

Spirits risen.

Reunion.

Face-to-face.

Celebrating their new arrival.

Thy mother's will be done.

Mallory traveled the cemetery path on stilted legs, her granddaughter's corpse held tight to her stained house dress with her right hand, a shovel dragging in her left. Her feet felt detached, propelled by someone else.

She needed to set things right.

You've gone way too far for that, dear, she thought. *There's no coming back from this. Cora will never forgive you. God will never forgive you. No wonder he won't answer your prayers.*

Her fate didn't matter. The baby deserved a proper burial. A resting place alongside their deceased family. There would be no eulogy, no poetry or flowery scripture to shuttle the child to her ancestors once she found a burial site. Mallory couldn't speak. Her lips refused to separate. She had no words, no thoughts to share.

The shovel's spade skipped on the rough path behind her. She didn't care. She had no energy to lift it.

Entering the cemetery, Mallory stopped to survey the configuration of the dead. Gravestones arranged in rows marked their dead, guiding the living through generations of grief. A strong wind swept through the trees, inciting a riot in the canopy surrounding the cemetery, the trees forming a welcoming committee of giants.

I can't put her in this ground, here in the open among our family. Cora will find her. She'll see the grave. That would be the end of her hope, the great eliminator, the revelation of Mallory's sin.

What else could she do? Hiding the child felt like a compounding offense Mallory couldn't stomach, couldn't afford. She wouldn't do it.

Movement at the far end of the circular clearing caught her eye. The sun's rays penetrating the treetops cast shadows to the treeline at the cemetery's edge. Mallory went to them, drawn by the flickering light. She felt eyes on her as she walked between the headstones. Her imagination was getting the best of her again. And she had good reason for her suspicion—she had a hard time trusting her reality.

She reached the end of the chosen row and stood idle, looking into the woods for several calming minutes. Her breathing slowed, her skin breaking out in tiny bumps as the cool breeze winding through the trees kissed her tacky skin. This was the resting place the child deserved.

Setting the infant on a bed of fallen leaves at her feet, Mallory kissed her fingers and pressed them to the baby's forehead. They were alone in that bitter, intimate moment, silence dominating the surrounding woods in a requiem to the recently departed. Turning to the woods, Mallory raised the shovel, drove the spade into the earth, and dug another grave.

The deafening silence of the surrounding woods persisted as Mallory stumbled down the cemetery path back to the house. The weight of her decisions, of the damage inflicted on their bloodline, pressed the life from her limbs and air from her lungs. She'd gone too far. No rational person could argue otherwise. The sweat and soil caked under her fingernails and into her cotton dress were damning evidence of her transgressions.

They'd never recover from this.

Mallory felt a tsunami of death roll from her, accelerating into a time beyond her reach, to unsuspecting, undeserving women down the line. A curse set like an immovable stone on their family.

"I'll never forgive you," she said aloud, hoping—*knowing*—Shadow Mother would hear her. The shovel spade emitted muted pings as it found small rocks in the peaks and valleys of the path unrolling behind her. Lacking the strength to carry the implement, she dragged it, wanting it as far from her as possible, an extension of her sinful work.

Your work isn't done yet. Shadow Mother's voice writhed and wormed through her head.

"I'm done."

Not quite. Ready your soul, woman.

Mallory stiffened against the threat, her legs cycling beneath her but seemingly in another reality. This place wasn't real, *couldn't* be reality.

On cue, the house emerged from behind the treeline. The looming white structure drew her forward, its gravitational pull aiding her return. Her daughter lay within its walls, awaiting her aid.

Mallory prepared her heart for battle. The time had come for confession, resolution.

CHAPTER 15

CORA

Sunlight warmed Cora's eyelids through her bedroom window. She lay still beneath her bedsheets, blinking away her sleep-cloaked vision and warped perception of time. She curled and uncurled her fingers and toes as her motor skills returned in misfires and fits. Waking felt unusually difficult, a foreign experience rather than a typical morning.

Is it morning?

Blinking to clear her vision, she looked around her room and back through the window for evidence of the time. Sunlight poured through the window at an angle more familiar to the afternoon but she couldn't determine the hour. She rubbed her eyes, struggling to gain more clarity, more understanding. She couldn't believe she'd slept so long.

The baby...

Cora couldn't recall when she'd last seen her newborn. *Had* she seen her?

Her! That's right! She'd given birth to a girl. How long had they been separated from each other? It couldn't have been long, the child must have fed from her...

But she couldn't recall feeding the baby. She remembered Mother feeding *her*, caring for *her*, but she couldn't conjure a single memory of feeding the child.

Could she feed? She'd heard of young mothers who struggled to produce milk for their babies resorting to cow's milk. Would Mother have fed the baby cow's milk rather than trouble her in her recovery? Regardless, she needed to get up, get going. She lolled her head to face the door but couldn't focus her eyes. The normally solid door bent and bobbed before her like a dancing sentry standing watch over her room.

I'm hallucinating, she thought. This realization brought a wave of concern to her scrambled thoughts. Everything felt wrong. Feeling precarious even while lying still, Cora didn't trust herself to move to the edge of her mattress yet. Worse yet, the thought of walking felt utterly impractical. She'd wait for Mother.

There's no reason to wait when you can call for her, she thought. Cora opened her mouth to call for Mother but produced an awkward, slurred *"muuuhhh"* instead. Like waking limbs, her tongue and lips lagged behind her brain, unable to form the word she normally said without effort.

Somewhere downstairs, a door opened and closed, rattling the walls. Perhaps Mother had returned from a trip to her garden. Cora tried to sit upright, but her vision spun uncontrollably, then settled again, prompting her to stay put. Panting and growing frustrated, she tried calling out for Mother again.

"Maaaaa."

This time her voice produced a more forceful sound. The footsteps crossing the hardwood floors downstairs paused in their pattern. Perhaps Mother had stopped to listen.

"Momma," she groaned louder, finally able to form a word, though her tongue still felt wrapped in cotton. She glanced at her nightstand hoping to find a glass of water. Instead, she found a stained doily and an unlit candelabra.

The footsteps resumed their rhythm, now transitioning to the stairs. Mother would arrive in her doorway any second now, eager to help Cora to her feet. Maybe she'd have the baby in her arms, a swaddled gift ready to welcome her back from her healing sleep.

The door slowly swung open on its protesting hinges. Blurry, clear, blurry again, the room came in and out of focus as Cora looked for Mother in the doorway.

Mother's face appeared first, peeking through the opening.

She looked...*horrible*.

Mother's eyes drooped with exhaustion, oily hair matted in places and wild in others. Streaks of red and brown soil stained her cheeks and forehead. Mother's teeth, dingy from years of drinking tea, stood like gravestones behind her cracked, parched lips.

Cora gasped. Mother noticed and ran one hand through her greasy hair as she pushed the door fully open with the other. As she stepped into the room, exposing her full form, Cora saw the damage Mother had done to her housedress, her unsuccessful attempt to scrub her hands free of the garden's soil, and the scrapes and scratches checking her veiny hands and forearms.

"I'm sorry to wake you, dear." Mother shuffled to the bed, barely lifting her feet with each step. She looked utterly depleted. She eased her bottom to the mattress's edge, nudging Cora aggressively but seemingly unaware of doing so. Her eyes fixed on the headboard just above Cora.

"Mother..." Cora tried to ask Mother what had happened, if she was okay, but she couldn't find the words.

She felt dizzy and unsettled, her stomach tumbling with hunger and soured contents. Foul body odor rolled from Mother in a warm wave, making matters for Cora's stomach worse.

Something was very wrong.

"Calm yourself, little lamb," Mother said. She took Cora's left hand in a sweaty grip, her hands trembling from too much use. Cora knew that feeling. Her hands trembled like that after a long day of labor with garden tools.

The moment felt wrong in every way. Mother shouldn't look so ill, and Cora shouldn't *feel* so poorly. Fear bubbled in Cora's gut and wrapped icy fingers around her pounding heart. A spike of adrenaline cleared her mind and steadied her vision. Cora tried to slip her hand from her mother's. Mother gripped tighter.

"Are you sick?" Cora didn't know what else to say.

Mother's face twisted as if to cry, then uncoiled, her trembling lips giving up her emotions. "I'm...not well, baby. But that's not what matters. I need to get you out of this bed and on your feet today. You're going to—"

"Where is my baby?" The words flew from Cora's mouth. She braced herself for Mother's response to the rude interruption. Unexpectedly, Mother kept her eyes on the headboard and continued her thought.

"You're going to struggle a bit today. We need to talk. But you're not ready yet. You've been bedridden for..." Mother paused, appearing to run through a calendar in her mind. Cora seized the opportunity.

"I'll be fine. I want to see her. Please, mother." She couldn't hold her emotions at bay, letting her tears slip down her cheeks.

Mother's stare dropped from the headboard and settled into Cora's upturned face. Cora saw her fear reflected in Mother's eyes.

"Please, Cora. I can't do this right now." Mother's words barely made it past her quaking lips. Her eyes dropped to her filthy hands, now empty and trembling in her lap.

"You're scaring me." Cora began to cry. "Where is my baby?"

"She..." Mother bounced her hands in her lap as tears poured from her swollen, bloodshot eyes. She looked up at the ceiling and took a deep breath. "She didn't make it."

Cora froze as the earth ground to a sudden, violent halt, casting reality askew. No more sound. No more words. An all-encompassing numbness separated her from the physical world. Before Cora, red-faced and utterly hysterical, Mother cried, her lips moving between webs of spit. But Cora heard nothing. She looked about the room, her vision shaken by Mother's erratic movement on the mattress beside her. Everything looked suddenly useless, meaningless. The row of books lining the top of her clothes dresser, stories she'd repeatedly read and adored over the years, meant nothing. Her dolls, sewn together in a patchwork of childhood memories and aged cloth, lay lifeless and flaccid in the wicker basket beside her small wooden desk. Their button eyes never contained life. They'd never been who she imagined them to be. Meaningless, all of them.

The sunlight streaming through her swaying sheer curtains had lost its heat, its energy ineffective and cold. Cora's spirit untethered from the useless things, thinned and contorted, and slipped into the dark cracks between the sun's rays, tumbling into a bottomless crevasse, end over end, into perpetual escape.

Into nothing.

CHAPTER 16
CORA

*I*vory moonlight illuminated the treetops behind the house. Swaying in the house's shadow, Cora stared into the woods. Eyes slightly squinted, she watched sprite shadows dart and dance between the towering trunks, carving smooth paths in the space between the physical and the spiritual.

She'd been there before, although she couldn't remember exactly when.

Cora couldn't recall the last time she had spoken or parted her lips. Nor did she remember having the urge to do so. Who would she speak to? She had been alone since Mother came home. Cora wished she'd stayed asleep, left to dream. Now, she stood in an unrivaled calm under the most comforting blanket of moonlight, physically desensitized but drowning in heartache.

Cora's head gradually tipped back, face pointing up, drawn by the power of the colossal moon. It appeared so impossibly close she couldn't comprehend the distance. Filling the night sky, the mammoth lunar body left little room for stars or the vastness of space. Closing her eyes, she begged the moon to heal her, to save her from the crushing weight of grief barreling down on her—an imminent threat, ready to pummel her into a million pieces with its brutality.

Mother spoke beside her. "We could bask in this power forever. Would you like that?"

Cora's heart broke into a sprint, cranking her nerves to heightened alert. Her eyes flew open, met first by that gloriously engorged moon. She dropped her chin and found herself inches from Mother's upturned face. Eyes closed, a smile pulling her features into a euphoric mask, Mother stood a breath away. Cora struggled to understand how Mother had arrived so stealthily.

"How—"

"Shhhhh. Just let me see..." Mother's voice trailed off. Then, her face lowered to meet Cora's. Mother opened her eyes, revealing two swirling pools of black liquid.

"Mother...your eyes." Reeling from the sight, Cora couldn't find words to describe her mother's affliction.

"Aren't they beautiful?" Mother smiled, shrugging her shoulders with giddiness.

"They're…"

"I have her, Cora. I have your little girl."

The breath fled Cora's lungs as if Mother had punched her in the stomach. "Where? Take me to her." Cora grabbed her mother's forearms below the elbows. As her fingers sank into Mother's tense flesh, a jolt of dread pulsed up her arms. This was all wrong. The spirits darting through the woods behind Mother whooped and howled like banshees. Cora couldn't understand their noises but she took them as a warning.

*"Gladly. But you must understand our–*circumstances.*"* *Mother's smile dropped from her stretched face. "She's mine now."*

"I don't understand. She's my *baby." Cora gripped her mother's arms more tightly, surely inflicting pain. Mother's slack face challenged her assumption.*

"Your mother gave her to me, Cora."

Your mother.

"I don't understand." Cora released her grip and pushed back from Mother as if her arms were vipers ready to strike.

"Maybe seeing is believing. Follow me." Mother turned and started down the path to the cemetery.

The ground fell out from under Cora's feet. Her body elevated from the earth and then stopped, perhaps pulled skyward by the overbearing moon. Without looking back,

Mother continued her journey onto the winding path, raising one hand to beckon her to follow. Cora's body complied under some foreign control. She opened her mouth to scream, but no sound came. She couldn't move, couldn't fight, unable to protest or flee. Her mouth remained tightly closed but her body moved forward, propelled by the unseen force. Rigid and shaking from the stimuli, Cora fell into line behind Mother. Her feet tipped forward, toes skipping across the ground as she floated in her mother's wake.

"Mmmmmmmmm!"

"Silence, child," Mother said. "The time to speak will come. For now, follow and listen. You sense me in her. You are keen. However, you cannot understand. She and I are one. We are inseparable."

Cora trembled in midair, groaning in rebellion as she coasted down the path behind Mother. Feral spirits whipped through the woods bordering the path, their manic cries filling the night air.

"This is all her fault, you know. She never intended to let you keep her. You broke her heart the day you revealed your sin. She had such high hopes for you. She knew the baby would divide you, pull your life inexorably into decline. People would judge you, speak ill of you behind your back. 'She's nothing but a whore'. And they'd be right, wouldn't they? Your child, the evidence, would support their claims.

But Mother wouldn't allow it. So, she gave her to me. She considered your heart for a moment but, truthfully, she barely put up a fight."

A war raged in Cora's immobile body. Ahead, the path merged with the cemetery clearing. Cora's anger and fear boiled over.

Why would she bring me here if she has my child?

Mother glanced over her shoulder, that goddamn smile pulling her cheeks in exaggerated angles.

"She's with me here, in this holy place. She's safe with me on this side, away from you and your sinful nature. You and your mother aren't fit to raise a child of our blood."

"Liar." Cora barely got the word out.

"Really? The baby didn't survive more than a few hours in your care. You two are weak."

Mother looked forward as she guided them between the rows of headstones. The markers glowed in the stark moonlight. They stopped near the clearing's edge, facing the woods.

Mother pointed.

"See for yourself, you ungrateful whore."

Cora fell from her suspended state, collapsing onto the grass. Lifting her head, she saw it.

There in the debris littering the forest floor, was a clearing—a grave.

Cora scrambled across the dewy grass on her hands and knees, passing directly through Mother, to the woods' edge.

"Stop!" Mother cried out. Cora's body went rigid once again, her eyes fixed on the small plot of cleared soil lying a few feet ahead in the darkness.

"My...baby," Cora said.

"Do you crave a reunion?" Mother asked.

"Yes! I'll do anything," Cora moaned.

"A child for a child," Mother replied.

"So be it." Cora had nothing to lose. No life to live on the other side.

"Then go to her," Mother said.

The reins of control released Cora's captive body. She crawled at breakneck speed, sharp twigs and fallen branches stabbing her palms and knees as she quickly closed the gap to the baby's freshly covered grave. As her hands plunged into the loosely packed soil, images assaulted her mind.

Mother's stained dress.

The clay caked on her forehead and cheeks.

This was her work.

She'd buried the child.

Cora went mad with rage, screaming through her clenched teeth, knowing she needed her child in her arms but also realizing she'd find no life in the baby's tiny body. Her screams excited the spirits in the woods, conjuring a paranormal riot among the trees. Glowing orbs flitted past her head, illuminating the scene and elongating shadows as they passed. Cora's eyes saw her hands work, but she couldn't register the moment in her mind, her brain blocking the heinous act from her memory.

Small birds, hidden from the moonlight by the thick canopy, dove and climbed in hectic patterns about her head.

The loose soil turned to thick clay in her hands, sticking to the crooks between her fingers, coating them in a natural layer of protection. Cora's sobs echoed from the earth to her ears.

Something soft, pliable, natural but entirely out of place, settled into Cora's cycling hands. She stopped, squeezed the tears from her eyes, and readied her heart for what came next.

She delivered her child from the soil.

Her baby, reborn.

Cora wiped the clay and loose dirt from the tiniest face she'd ever seen.

Perfect lips.

A nose so small the tip of her pinky matched its width.

Lovely porcelain skin reflecting the moonlight where the soil had fallen away.

She was perfect.

She was hers.

Mother approached, looking down on Cora with eyes as black as coal tar pitch.

"Isn't she precious?"

Cora's rage stoked hotter. This was Mother's work. How dare she?

"I never want to see you again," Cora spat.

"Fair. But we had a deal—a child for a child."

Cora looked down into her child's lifeless face. Her heart fluttered, aching on the edges of each beat.

"You'll give her back to me? Forever?"

Mother nodded, her onyx eyes flashing in the moonlight. "Forever."

"A child for a child," Cora confirmed.

Mother's smile relaxed as she turned her palms up to the sky. Two dark aerodynamic bodies dropped from the canopy to her hands, starlings with glistening black eyes to match Mother's.

"Raise your palms as I have," Mother said.

Cora hesitated, afraid to set her baby back to the earth, fearing she'd somehow lose her again.

"Do it," Mother commanded.

Cora did as she was told. She laid the baby on the ground before her folded knees, sat upright, and raised her open palms. The starlings flew to her, their sharp talons finding purchase in her tender palms. Cora's heartbeat ran away like an ungoverned engine. Her arms sagged as the starlings settled into her hands, peering down over her bent wrists.

The pecking began gently at first, then more forcefully, hammering, driving pointed beaks into supple, paper-thin skin. Blood ran down Cora's wrists and forearms in rivulets, then rivers. She pulled her arms closer, instinctively trying to evade the pain. The starlings dug their claws into her hands, increasing the speed of their strikes, blood now speckling her face, bedclothes, arms, and thighs. Cora squeezed her eyes shut, blocking out the image of the birds destroying her wrists. Her head pounded alarms...

STOP THIS STOP THIS STOP THIS

She felt warm blood run in steady streams down both arms, pouring into her lap, and becoming tacky in the humid Virginia night air. Without warning, both starlings leaped from her hands, their wings beating the air before her face.

Cora opened her eyes. Her wrists appeared like two bloody mouths staring back at her. Cora's heart pounded harder, forcing surges of blood to gush in torrents from each gaping wrist.

Oh no.

Mother knelt beside Cora and extended one open hand toward the baby lying before her.

"*Feed her.*"

Cora nodded, understanding her time was drawing to a close. She reached for her baby, her crimson arms dripping blood to the surrounding leaves. Cradling the child in her left arm, she pressed her hemorrhaging right wrist to the baby's lips. Cora's life poured down the child's chin and neck, pooling above her shoulders momentarily before draining.

"That's good," Mother said, her eyes wide churning pools of endless dread. "Rest with her."

Cora's head swam as she braced herself with her right hand and lowered her body to the forest floor. She pulled the baby tight to her, pressing their foreheads together. Cora closed her eyes, and Mother stroked her hair.

"You've done well, child. You've kept your promise, and I'll keep mine. She's yours now in eternal slumber. My girls. The first of many. You've done well."

Cora's eyelids grew heavy, raising and lowering with each heartbeat. She kept her eyes fixed on her daughter. Her precious...

"Clara. My precious Clara."

Beckoned, Clara opened her eyes to the night, glistening blue jewels sparkling with reflected moonlight. Cora smiled, her heart swelling with pride and love. As Clara's mouth moved deeper into her feeding wrist, Cora whispered, "The dark doesn't stand a chance against us."

Content for the first time in her brief life, Cora silently rejoiced as the shadows pulled her from life into eternity.

CHAPTER 17

MALLORY

"A child for a child."

Shadow Mother's voice ripped Mallory from a dreamless sleep. She gasped as she sat up, pulling her sheets tight to her chest in terror.

Standing at the foot of her bed, Shadow Mother resembled a charcoal smear against the darkness of her unlit room. Black tendrils rolled from her form like smoke riding an imperceptible breeze. Her eyes glimmered as a new band of moonlight streamed through the bedroom window.

"That girl of yours is special. A woman of her word."

Mallory's muscles tightened while she considered all the potential meanings in Shadow Mother's words.

"You leave Cora alone."

Shadow Mother huffed. "You never have to worry about that again."

Mallory's pulse pounded in her ears, thrumming through her arteries with each contraction of her heart. Her fear rose several notches.

"What have you done?"

"I kept my promise."

Mallory launched from the bed in a white blur, blowing past Shadow Mother into the upstairs hallway. Cora's bedroom door stood open at the end of the hallway, but she'd shut it before retiring for the night.

Time slowed to a cruel, grueling pace as Mallory's bare feet screeched across the hardwood floors, her hands gripping the door frame to arrest her momentum. Cora's bedsheets lay strewn across the floor.

"No! Cora!"

Mallory spun on her heels and lunged for the bathroom door. But Cora wasn't there either.

Mallory ran for the stairs, the balls of her feet barely grazing the steps as she descended the stairs in a flash. Crashing into the wall across from the stairs, she spun left for the front of the house.

Cora wasn't in the sitting room or the family room. Back in the main hall, Mallory looked toward the rear of the house, to the back door opposite the kitchen table.

The door stood open.

Cora. The cemetery. The baby.

Mallory ran for the back door, feeling it stretch away from her, growing distant with each step like a cruel trick in a nightmare. Her legs carried her, but she couldn't feel them beneath her. She floated through the door, across the porch, and onto the yard, the sound of her sobs now echoing off the trees and house in the silent night.

She couldn't run fast enough. Sharp breaths inflicted pain in her lungs, and her brain tipped on the edge of consuming too much oxygen. Her panic broke through her defenses, overcame her control, and crushed her perception of reality.

This isn't real. I'm dreaming, she thought.

Rather than a replying voice, the anxious sense of dread pinballing between her stomach, chest, and brain proved this was *too* real.

Now on the cemetery path, Mallory screamed for her daughter in a shrill, manic voice.

"Cora! Don't!"

Don't what? Don't look? Don't find your baby's grave?

Don't dig her up.

Mallory reached a point of helplessness that made her want to stop running and simply accept what would come. She couldn't change what had happened, couldn't take any of it back. No matter what she did, Mallory couldn't escape her sins.

She stumbled into the cemetery clearing like an apparition, glowing in the cool moonlight, her nightgown flowing to the wet grass sullying her bare feet. She looked toward the baby's burial site, but from that distance in the dark shadows of the trees, Mallory couldn't find Cora standing in mourning. Perhaps she'd been mistaken.

Maybe I'm dreaming. Maybe Cora is still upstairs in her bed.

No, this was real. She was there in the cemetery, her body overheating from sprinting, her feet sore and throbbing, her—

Mallory's feet jammed to the earth, stopping her several yards from the edge of the trees. There, beneath the oaks and maples, Cora nestled her baby beside the grave in the woods. Rays of filtered moonlight painted white stripes across their maroon bodies. Cora's dried blood covered mother and child, like a second layer of shadows. There was so much—*too much*—blood. Mallory couldn't process the image.

Mallory wanted to scream Cora's name, to rip her from the ground and into her arms, but she couldn't move. Her mind refused to accept what she saw. Swaying in shock, the moment broke her spirit, decomposing her soul, scattering her essence to the cemetery breeze, destroying her, leveling her history from birth to this point, this penance for her tragic life, her indiscretions.

Her lips started trembling first, then her hands. She tried to scream, to cast her voice into the night and wake every living creature, to wake the dead, but her mouth remained shut. Instead, a guttural, horrifying groan started in her bowel, climbed into her chest, and vibrated from her throat. She fell to her knees beside them, awash in a grief so substantial it stunned Mallory's physical body. Deep inside, the embers of grief smoldered with the intensity of a thousand suns.

Cora was gone.

"You did this. You killed them."

Mallory must have said the words. They came from her thoughts and she heard them with her ears, but she couldn't feel her mouth moving. She waited for a response from Shadow Mother. Silence prevailed. The cemetery remained in complete, damning silence.

Shadow Mother didn't appear beside her, did not come to brag or harass her in her time of utter defeat.

Mallory stood alone. She'd hurt everyone she'd ever loved. Destroyed them. She deserved her silence, the judgment of her maker.

Where was her God?

With the innocent.

Mallory stood there for hours looking up at the night sky and talking with her dead family. She spoke mostly with her mother and father. Of course, she exchanged difficult words with her husband. But as the sky breaching the cemetery clearing took on its purple hue, a calm settled on her broken heart. She knew what she had to do. But first, she wanted to watch the sunrise with her daughter one last time before she buried her.

Mallory left the cemetery shortly after the sun broke over the trees, dragging her shovel across the winding path for the last time. She'd said her goodbyes, made whatever peace she could with herself as she worked.

It'd never be enough.

Entering the back porch, she leaned the shovel against the door frame, took one look over her shoulder to her beloved garden, then entered the house.

Her footsteps echoed through the home as she moved through it. The place was devoid of life. No sound of Cora stirring in her room as she started her day. No movement in the kitchen as Mallory prepared their breakfast.

Nothing.

Reaching the stairs, Mallory set one filthy hand on the banister and one muddy foot on the bottom step, then stopped.

Wet footprints painted each step before her. Mallory smiled and followed.

Reaching the upstairs landing, she stopped to look in Cora's room. She'd cherished every moment with her girl there.

Combing her hair before school.

Reading Aesop's fables to the tiny body tucked beneath the sheets each night.

A life well-lived.

Mallory closed her eyes, straining to relive those memories there in the hall, to hear Cora's childish voice one more time. She felt the warmth on her exposed arms before she heard their voices, but they eventually came. Laughter and mumbles, childhood "I love you's" and tickle giggles.

My God, what a wonderful feeling!

She could stay there forever. And she would.

But first, Mallory needed to wash up. She stepped into the adjacent bathroom, still buzzing from the voices in the hall. Closing the door behind her, she called out, "I'll be out in a minute, baby!"

Her feet found the wet footprints Cora had tracked around the tile floor after her bath. No matter how many times she told her, the girl refused to dry off completely in the tub. Mallory wished she had a dime for every wet footprint she'd stepped on over the years. But it was just another wonderful way to experience her daughter, so she hid her smiles when she griped at Cora.

Mallory looked at her filthy arms in disbelief. How had she made such a mess of herself in the garden? She'd ruined her nightgown as well. Hopefully, she could scrub the stains out. She slipped out of the gown, letting it pool around her feet on the tile floor before stepping gingerly to the tub to run the water.

The tub was already full.

Mallory stood in disbelief, one hand lingering on the hot water valve. Perhaps Cora had seen her returning from the garden and ran the bath for her.

A painful cramp shot through Mallory's right forearm. She yanked her hand back from the valve. Rubbing her sore muscles with her other hand, she stepped into the tub, relishing the heat prickling her calves. Sore and weary, she lowered her body fully into the tub.

She couldn't remember the last time she'd bathed, let alone had a moment to *enjoy* a bath. Motherhood demanded so much from her, she rarely had time to enjoy simple pleasures such as a hot, restorative bath. Mallory gave herself over to the relaxing heat, closing her eyes, and sinking up to her mouth in the water.

A gentle knock at the door.

Mother entered, her hair pinned expertly, not a strand out of place. Her blue dress swayed elegantly about her as she turned to shut the door.

Mallory's tiny body bobbed in the water, barely below the surface. The bubbles she'd made with the soap were almost gone now. A few spherical bodies floated across the surface inches from her face. She raised her head out of the water enough to hear Mother. From the stern look on her face, Mallory doubted she'd like this conversation.

"Little one, you've made a terrible mess of things."

Mallory spat the water from her lips. "I'm sorry."

"Sorry's not good enough this time." Mother's mouth normally scrunched together when she was angry, but she appeared to be holding back a smile.

Mallory smiled back, testing Mother's resolve.

"Finish your bath. I'll be waiting for you."

A fun smirk broke Mother's steely resolve, filling Mallory with relief. Mother turned and flipped the light off as she left. A thin band of light glowed in the gap under the door. Mallory loved bathing in the dark. This was another of Mother's subtle gifts.

Stretching her body to its full length in the tub, Mallory imagined bobbing on the ocean under the night sky. The stars glistening and sparkling in the perfect dome above her filled her with an unrivaled sense of wonder. She'd never seen such a brilliant display at night.

A universe lay before her, a vast, timeless expanse full of mysteries. She wondered if Heaven was up there.

"Want to find out?" Mother's voice came to her from the water.

Mallory nodded, excited yet hesitant. She stared into a sky so big she feared she'd get lost in it. Would she drift forever in the frigid darkness between the stars?

"The dark doesn't stand a chance against us," Mother said.

Mallory nodded one last time before Mother's arms wrapped around her tiny body and pulled her into forever.

ACT III

1986

CHAPTER 18

ABIGAIL

Cora's fingers fell from Abigail's tear-streaked face, drawing her from the vision and back to the present. No longer held by Cora's spell, Abigail sat hard and let sorrow's elixir pass through her heart. She needed time to process all she'd experienced of Cora and Mallory. Their story, heartbreaking and illuminating, explained so much about what Abigail and Constance had experienced in the house—in the family.

Their house wasn't haunted.

They were haunted.

"Abi?" Constance and Adeline were no longer held captive by whatever—*whoever*—had overcome them once their digging had paid off. They sat to her left, outside the grave, their eyes glassy and faces tight with worry.

Abigail nodded to show Constance she was okay. She couldn't speak, didn't know how to respond to what she'd witnessed through Cora's visions. Abigail met Cora's blinking eyes again.

According to Cora's visions, she'd been reunited with Clara in her death, then buried together. So, where was Clara?

"Your baby...Clara. Where is she?"

Cora pointed to the clouded sky. A murmuration of starlings painted erratic patterns against the backdrop of clouds above them. Abigail contemplated what the birds represented. Each of the women of the Whispering House possessed a starling, a victim lost to this curse.

Mallory had Cora.

Cora had Clara.

Lydia had Adeline.

Delilah had Constance.

And Constance was fighting to keep Abigail alive.

But according to Cora's visions, she'd been reunited with Clara in her death. Mallory had buried them together. Abigail sat in their grave as she contemplated these mysteries, the child's body nowhere in sight. Abigail seriously doubted the child had reincarnated, soul and physical body, into a bird.

The mystery expanded in Abigail's mind. She'd met Lydia, Adeline, Constance, her mother, and now Cora in their afterlife. Where were Mallory and Clara? Perhaps a heaven existed beyond the afterlife Constance and Adeline had found. Maybe for Clara. The newborn was the purest among them, unblemished and sinless—an innocent child. And Constance and Adeline had insisted they'd seen Cora and Clara laying together in the woods, but not in the same state as the other spirits.

Maybe Mallory was in Hell. Abigail didn't want that to be true. In many ways, Mallory was a victim like the others—manipulated, traumatized, and haunted. Could she really adopt the mantle of guilt for what she'd done or was she simply a pawn, terrorized by whatever Shadow Mother was?

As the lines connected and crossed in Abigail's mind, she became more convinced they needed to find their missing girls and end this haunting, this curse afflicting the women of their family.

Abigail glanced between the hovering ghosts of Constance and Adeline toward the cemetery path and sensed the house's gravitational pull. They were close to liberating their bloodline. Perhaps she'd finally found her purpose in life. She felt genuinely motivated for the first time in years. She'd lived her life running from this curse.

No more.

Pulling her attention back to the cemetery, she looked at Cora.

"We'll find Clara. And your mother. And we'll finally take care of Shadow Mother."

Constance shook her head. "I'm not sure that's a good idea. Think about the damage she's done to this family. We're all dead. You're the last of us."

Abigail wasn't surprised by Constance's warning. Connie was her protector; she always would be.

"That's exactly why she needs to be stopped. And I've got nothing to lose. I've already lost everyone I love," Abigail said.

"What about *your* life?" Constance asked as she stood.

Joining Constance, Adeline rose to her feet. Brushing the dirt from her ghostly hands, she looked rejuvenated, maybe even excited.

"I'm with you, Abi. We finally found Cora. Now we find Mallory and the baby and end this."

Constance shook her head in disagreement. "After all we've learned about Shadow Mother? She almost killed you in the tub this morning, Abi. She's extremely dangerous to the living. Remember?"

Cora gripped Abigail's right hand. "I'm with you. Help me find my mother. She needs me."

Abigail looked up from the grave to Constance's concerned face, then back to Cora. "Where do we start?"

Cora grabbed Abigail firmly by both arms. "With you."

"Me? I don't understand."

"I see Shadow Mother festering in you like a sickness."

A heat spread through Abigail's body, an expanding sense of guilt—like she'd been caught holding a vile secret. Anger followed, building momentum in her body. But she had no reason to be angry. Conflicted, she struggled to understand her reaction.

"I see her in your face," Cora said.

"And what exactly do you plan to do, little lamb?" Abigail heard the words leave her mouth but in someone else's voice. She understood them, recalling the nickname Mallory had given Cora. But they were not her words to speak.

Cora's eyes narrowed into slits. Constance and Adeline protested behind her, their words muddled, meaningless noises to Abigail's ears.

Now fully under the control of a pilot she couldn't name, Abigail straddled the wasting pine box and bore down on Cora. Heat rolled from her skin like the warmth of a radiator in the dead of winter.

Constance's voice broke through. "Leave my sister alone!"

Abigail—*Shadow Mother*—turned around to face the ghosts of her sister and cousin. She raised her hands like a conductor prompting her orchestra for the first note of a piece, then she dropped her arms.

Constance and Adeline collapsed into the earth as if pulled back to their graves by tethers. Cora screamed behind her but Abigail didn't fret. Instead, she turned back to Cora, her hands still raised, threatening to repeat the same act.

Cora was gone, no longer lying in the box between Abigail's feet. Staring down into the muddy hole she'd created, Abigail's stomach lurched, then something exploded up through her esophagus, flooding her mouth with a river of liquid charcoal. The black stream blasted from her mouth and nose, filling her eyes with acidic tears.

Someone wrapped their hands in her hair and yanked her backward with brutal force. Leaving her feet, Abigail flew face up to the churning clouds, the world grinding to a halt. Weightless and relieved from the sensation of violent vomiting, she soared backward and out of Cora's shallow grave.

Time stood still.

Abigail hovered, suspended above the cemetery, rigid and defenseless. A dark, angry sky met her gaze, treetops swaying rhythmically at the perimeter. Muscles spasming,

Abigail slowly rotated upright, the cemetery coming into view again.

The surrounding woods came alive, voices surging in a cacophony of indecipherable shouts and cries as shadows emerged from behind trees. Some shot about in dark streaks, others lumbered painstakingly toward the cemetery clearing.

Abigail knew this alternate plane, the dark realm between life and death, the place from her visions and dreams. It was here now, her worlds merging.

The cemetery: a place where the dead came forward.

Abigail had never feared her gift, even as a young child, likely because she'd never *not* seen the dead. She was a pre-teen when she realized she was the only person she knew who had the gift. Only then did she realize how abnormal her experience was.

But now, outnumbered many times over and lacking control over her body, she feared her gift.

The familiar faces of Mrs. Harting and Steph, her dead friend from school, emerged from the pack of spirits coalescing at the interface between the cemetery and the forest.

"You should have joined us peacefully when you had the chance, dear. I fear this route will be much worse," Mrs. Harting said, sighing in disappointment. Abigail's pulse throbbed in her wrists beneath her healing suicide slits, reminding her to no longer trust Mrs. Harting.

"We tried. We *all* tried." Steph drew a hitched breath. "Why wouldn't you listen?"

Abigail couldn't move her mouth to reply. Instead, a garbled groan rattled through her throat. Regret seized her. They were right; they'd all tried to help her and she'd ignored them, persisting in the fight to reclaim a home destined to kill her.

But they didn't understand—she'd *had* to finish what they'd started. She'd fought to liberate her mother and to show Constance love when no one else could. She'd tried to breathe life back into their home when the rest of the world refused them.

And now the threads of pain, struggle, and intentions wove into a multigenerational tapestry. She was the last of her bloodline, the final resistance against the evil curse that had wiped them out.

And her enemy now formed before her in Cora's grave, a black column building on itself in the muddy pit, materializing into the silhouette of a woman. The column built higher, roughly six feet tall now, rippling and popping like boiling tar. Arms extended from the twisting core. A head took shape, bearing minimal facial features. As a mouth warped into shape, its lips parted, fluid bubbling between the thick folds. An earthy, caustic stench blew over Abigail in an unsettlingly hot breeze. Hair sprouted from the scalp in rigid, straw-like strands before laying flat and smoothing past elegantly swept shoulders.

Shadow Mother opened her eyes and surveyed the messy grave beneath her. Terror consumed Abigail.

"My girl, look at the mess you've made." Shadow Mother lifted her gaze, her head still tipped downward. "I gave you every opportunity to join us, you ungrateful *bitch*."

The last word stung like a slap across Abigail's face. "You...killed them."

"No, dear. I showed them eternal love. And now you'll see that love for yourself. In *our* house, of course." Shadow Mother pointed down the cemetery path to her childhood home. "This is the end of your story. It's time to go home."

The dead bordering the cemetery howled and screamed.

Mrs. Harting hollered, "Take her home!"

Steph repeated the phrase like a macabre cheerleader, "Take her home! Take her home!" Black spit as thick as tar poured from her mouth and down her chin as she screamed the words.

Shadow Mother raised her arms as Abigail had done before banishing Constance, Adeline, and Cora to the earth.

"No! Please!" Abigail pleaded.

Shadow Mother smiled, tipped her head to one side, and dropped her arms like twin guillotine blades.

Abigail flew into the open grave, cast into impenetrable darkness—then opened her eyes to the sounds of screams in the upstairs hall of the Whispering House.

CHAPTER 19

ABIGAIL

Abigail cried out as she crashed into the wall outside her bedroom and collapsed onto the hardwood floor. Lying face down in the hallway she'd traversed countless times in her youth, she struggled to regain the breath knocked from her lungs. Despite the pain and discomfort, she was grateful to be alive. Considering Shadow Mother's past, she thought things could have ended much worse for her.

Gasping for air like a fish out of water, Abigail pressed her hands to the floor and pushed herself upright. Her ears rang from the collision, but she heard a woman scream at the soft edges of the static.

Abigail blinked to clear her vision in the dark, her emotions bound in a knot threatening to unravel as she braced herself against the wall with one hand and struggled to her feet.

My god, those screams.

They came at her from all directions, emanating from every room of the house. Not one woman screaming, but several.

The volume grew as the ringing subsided and her hearing returned. There was no mistaking the sounds—anguished, gut-wrenching sobs. She heard her mother's cries first, somewhere downstairs, then another woman's, familiar yet unidentifiable.

A new sound broke through the tortured chorus and pulled her fully into the moment—a body thrashing in the tub on the opposite side of the wall beneath her hand.

"Adeline."

Abigail stumbled toward the end of the hall where her bedroom and the bathroom doors faced each other. With every unsteady step, the thrashing and sobbing intensified. Without warning, her left knee buckled, sending her stumbling into the wall bordering her room. The screams rose to a nerve-shattering crescendo.

Abigail squeezed her eyes shut and called out in despair. "I'm coming! I'm so sorry!"

She sensed this was all her fault. Whatever hell waited for her in those rooms, whatever tormented the souls of the women of the Whispering House, their pain was her fault. She'd crossed the line this time. She'd antagonized their oppressor and stoked the flames of their demise.

A sudden torrent of vomit exploded from Abigail's mouth. Thick black tar spilled from her in an aggressive eruption. Eyesight blurred with tears, her left foot slipped in the emulsion, causing her to crash to the floor in a brutal tangle of quivering limbs and convulsing muscles. Abigail landed on her left side, moaning and desperate to get back on her feet. To reach the women crying out for her. Sticky black vomit coated her palms as she clawed her way back to her hands and knees and crawled as fast as she could to the landing outside the opposing doors. She stopped between them, momentarily paralyzed with fear and indecision. She had to choose one to open first, a decision made more difficult by the horrifying wails behind each door.

Abigail watched as the doors to her childhood bedroom and the hall bath slowly opened in unison, revealing similar but separate scenes of utter heartbreak and hellish entrapment.

In her room, Cora's corpse lay in her—*their*—bed, her white nightgown and bedsheets soaked through with gore. The teen's lips looked purple and bruised against her pallid, dead skin. Sitting in a wooden chair in the far corner of the room, staring flatly at her dead daughter, Mallory pressed a muddy bundle of baby and cotton to her bosom. Mallory's sobs came out like a long, deep *buuuuuuh*. Her slack facial muscles, hanging jaw, and half-closed eyes implied she'd been awake and crying for a hundred years.

Abigail needed to stop this, to defeat Shadow Mother once and for all. Their family's grief and trauma were long overdue for revenge.

A waterborne struggle played out behind her, beyond the bathroom door, the vicious backing track to a mother's desperate cries. Abigail turned on her heels and stepped to the open bathroom door, physically unable to penetrate the threshold and interfere with Lydia's grief. Hands clawing through the churning water, Lydia knelt beside her thrashing daughter's body in the tub, trying desperately to arrest the violence and draw Adeline to the surface. Her hands plunged into the water then came up empty, her frantic eyes skipping across the peaks and valleys of the undulating water. Back in they went, grasping for limbs, for the luckiest snag of hair, for the slick, warm skin of a panicked, drowning child. A recycled death just out of reach on a horrifying loop.

Lydia's face twisted into one expression after another like the worst slideshow imaginable. First, tight desperation. Then, shuddering disbelief breaking over to helpless panic, followed by inconceivable grief. Through it all, her mumbles, screams, and prayers gave her hell a voice.

Abigail tried to step in, to enter the scene and render aid. In her mind, she plunged into the tub, wrapped her cousin in her arms, and stood with her limp body held tight to her chest. Black water poured from them as gravity pulled death's weapon back to the endless abyss beneath them. She presented Adeline's small body to her manic mother like a prize fish plucked from the ocean.

But in reality, Abigail did nothing. She couldn't move. Some force kept her from breaching the threshold, from stopping Lydia's and Adeline's endless pain. Unable to physically interact with them, Abigail felt like a casual witness to the worst moment in someone else's life, to an unstoppable nightmare sequence.

"Aunt Lydia...I can't help...I can't move...I'm sorry...I..."

Abigail felt like a calf tangled in an electric fence. A thousand angry, squeezing hands held her in painful suspension in the doorway.

You're the reason for their suffering. See the hell you've caused. Shadow Mother's voice passed through her in a violating whisper, careful not to give her a reprieve from the screams and cries echoing through the house.

And it worked. A jagged spike of guilt penetrated her core and bloomed like a mushroom cloud. She'd refused to comply, to give herself over fully to death, always pulling back, allowing her soul to rebound to life when the opportunity came amid the chaos.

I did it for Connie. I chose life for her, she thought. But at what price? She'd refused Shadow Mother's last prize and plotted to end her reign. Now she was forced to watch, helpless and guilty, as the women of her bloodline suffered.

"Constance!" Her mother cried from downstairs, ripping her from her thoughts and into action.

"My God, nononono..." Abigail panicked.

Lunging backward to escape the bathroom doorway, nearly tumbled down the stairs when she broke free. Abigail regained her balance and scrambled down the stairs, her slick bare feet slipping over the steps as she flew toward her mother's voice, leaving the tormented souls in her room and the bathroom behind for now.

The sitting room!

Abigail swung hard on the banister, rocketing herself toward the front foyer on numb legs. At the edge of her vision, she saw water dripping from the ceiling. Abigail fought off the memories of their last escape from the house, black water raining on them as Shadow Mother pursued them.

Ahead, starlings darted through a thickening cloud of rancid smoke between the opening of the sitting room and the adjacent living room.

"Mama! Connie!"

Abigail knew what hellish gift awaited when she reached the archway to the sitting room, but there was no turning back now. No avoiding a confrontation with the worst day of her life. As she neared the opening on her left, the glow of her sister's burning body illuminated the walls.

Time slowed as Abigail stumbled fully into the archway and squared her body to the scene unfolding in the sitting room. A wall of heat stole the breath from her lungs and attacked the bare skin on her arms, neck, and face.

A mammoth fire raged in the center of the room. In the heart of the flames, a fuel to consume for eternity, Constance stood defiantly, arms out to her sides, body rolling in waves of orange and yellow light. Her mother lay pinned to the couch on the left side of the room, limbs splayed to shield the child beneath her. Abigail glimpsed her young legs coiled tight beneath her mother's protection. Delilah's wide eyes and blistering face threatened to burst into flames in the unbearable heat rolling from Constance's burning body.

Mama had been forced to save her youngest, and consequently, to leave her firstborn to the flames.

"Oh, Mama." Her lips quaked as her mother's unbearable heartache settled into Abigail's racing heart. Even under the protection of death, as a ghost free of life's unavoidable pain, her mother had faced the impossible decision to save one child over another. Delilah looked at her, tears drying on her face in the intense heat.

"I chose you, Abigail. And what have you done to repay me? You've chased death and trapped me and the rest of your family in an endless cycle of pain. Free us."

Abigail saw regret in her mother's terrified eyes. She saw a life of love and dedication lost to flame. They'd been taken from each other, all of them, far too soon. Abigail hadn't truly lived since her mother's death. She'd tried to give Constance a life in a twisted purgatory of ghostly existence but that lie ran its course and eventually reality tore them apart again. They'd been fighting nature for too long.

Delilah slowly pulled her arms and legs back to her center and stood from the couch. She leaned down and scooped her frightened daughter from the couch, tucking young Abigail's legs around her hips, and smoothing her head to her strong, motherly shoulder.

Standing in the doorway, Abigail nodded, accepting what felt inevitable. She wanted this to end, *craved* eternal resolution for her family regardless of the cost.

Delilah stepped around the burning coffee table and across the room, stopping before Abigail in the archway. Behind her, Constance collapsed to the floor, the flames intensifying as they licked her tender flesh. Abigail groaned at the finality of the sight, wanting to go to Constance in the flames, to lie beside her sister and give herself over. Delilah stepped closer, obstructing her view. She gently took Abigail's right hand by the wrist and laid it on the child draped over her shoulder. Abigail felt her young heartbeat beneath her aged fingers and everything loosened inside her, *around* her. The screams from Lydia and Mallory upstairs grew tinny and distant, lost to the connection Abigail felt with her young self, with the beating heart of an innocent child held in her mother's protection.

True love.

Starlings shot like missiles in and out of the archway above Abigail's head, tempting the flames but turning away at the last second, before the heat could consume their feathered bodies and hollow bones. Abigail understood their message—to avoid the flames, to seek safety.

"I'd protect you again if I could, baby. I'd scoop you up in my arms and shield you from the flames. Maybe that's what this is."

Mama moved Abigail's hand from the girl's back to her own face. Abigail couldn't breathe, touching her mother's warm cheek again for the first time in twenty years. Her hand moved from Mother's cheek to her mouth where supple lips placed loving kisses along the backs of her sore fingers. Abigail began to cry, quietly but deeply. She couldn't peel her eyes from Delilah's.

"I miss you so much, Mama."

"I know, baby. It's okay. We can make this work. You can stay here as long as you'd like. We'll make it beautiful."

Abigail nodded, letting her tears run uninterrupted down her grimy face.

"No more running. No more pain." Mama looked over her shoulder to Constance writhing in flames on the floor behind her, then back to Abigail. "No more death."

"How? How do I help them?" Abigail wanted the pain to end, to move past this hell and return to beauty. She wanted to nestle against Mama's beautiful face forever.

"Through love." Mama's tears spilled over Abigail's fingers. She pushed her cheek into Abigail's palm, pressing further until Abigail's hand was sandwiched between her mother's cheek and the comforted child's back. It felt like a full-circle moment for Abigail.

Mama straightened her neck and freed Abigail's hand. "Come, there's something I want to show you."

Abigail recoiled. "But what about Constance? We need to help her."

Mama stepped past Abigail without responding. As she walked down the hall toward the rear of the house, the child, young Abigail from twenty years ago, looked up from her mother's shoulder.

Black vomit seeped from between the girl's lips.

CHAPTER 20

ABIGAIL

Abigail looked from her mother walking down the hall to her sister's charred body in the sitting room.

"I won't go with you."

Delilah stopped, facing away from Abigail.

"You're not my mama. Mama protected me. She wanted me to live. And my sister wanted me to live. Everyone wanted me to live. Everyone but *you*."

Above Delilah, Abigail noticed a change on the dripping ceiling through the smoke. The droplets, now various shades of gray and black, ran together before dripping to the floor in thick globs, too viscous to be water.

She looked down at the black stains on her shirt from her repeated bouts of sickness and again at the black vomit coating the small chin of the child clinging to her mother's ghost in the hall.

She wanted none of what Mama offered. This house, this existence, wasn't beautiful. It was awful.

"I don't trust you." Abigail steadied her swaying legs and prepared for confrontation. She drew a deep breath. "You're *not* my mother."

Delilah's hair, flowing chestnut waves spilling down her back, shook first, telegraphing the anger racking the woman's body. Still facing away, she guided young Abigail down from her shoulder and set her on her feet in the hall.

Young Abigail's face looked odd, her features distorted at the edges. She pleaded with her mother to pick her back up.

"Please, Mother." The girl's arms extended upward, bent in awkward angles at the elbows.

"Not now. Mother must fix this." Standing at the base of the stairs, Delilah turned to face Abigail. Blood as thick and dark as black paint poured down her face in long rivulets. Beside her, young Abigail's extended arms bent backward on themselves. Her arms and legs hinged and folded in unnatural angles, skin opening and spilling dark liquid.

Abigail tried to block the images of her young body contorting from settling into her memory, from resurfacing in future nightmares. But she couldn't pry her eyes from the coalescing pile of viscera and bone collecting at her mother's side.

Shaking with barely repressed anger, Delilah looked back at Abigail. "Look what you've done. You ruin *everything*."

"No! *You* ruin everything. You've ruined all of us!" Abigail screamed hysterically. "You're not my mother. You'll *never* be my mother. You're a curse. A scourge."

Delilah's quaking body peeled away from the Shadow Mother contained within. Her flesh sloughed away effortlessly, coiling into black tendrils and merging with the billowing smoke pouring down the hall from the sitting room.

Shadow Mother stood before Abigail as she had in the cemetery, her true form on display in all its horrible detail.

"I tried to do this gently, you stubborn, ungrateful wretch. But if you prefer pain over pleasure, I'll gladly oblige."

Abigail tried to formulate a witty retort, whip up a response to show Shadow Mother she was ready to stand and fight, but she couldn't think past the primal fear crippling her faculties.

"Feel their pain if you must," Shadow Mother said. "You'll fold, eventually. And when you do, I'll be there to snatch you into death."

Acting on instinct and blind faith, Abigail turned and ran for the front door. Bringing the fight to this house had been a terrible mistake, one that would surely cost her life. She'd tried to take a stand in the cemetery and failed, giving Shadow Mother the advantage and opportunity to bring the fight to her high ground. To bring it to the Whispering House. Abigail needed an opportunity she couldn't identify, an ally she couldn't name, *any* advantage. Shadow Mother was right; if she stayed and fought, Abigail wouldn't last long.

Eyes fixed on the front door, she ran from Shadow Mother, from the amplified screams of Lydia and Mallory and the silent suffering of Constance, Adeline, Cora, Clara, and Delilah. As she reached the archway leading to the sitting room, something caught her eye, distracting her from the front door and altering her plan of escape. Without thinking, Abigail dove through the archway and snatched the portrait of Aunt Lydia and Adeline from the floor beside her sister's burning body.

Abigail felt something change in the house, heard movement in its bones like an old skeleton stretching its decomposing sinews. Doors opened and slammed in their frames upstairs. A deep groan filled the sitting room.

Shadow Mother cried out in the hall.

Struggling to inhale after knocking the wind from her lungs in the fall, Abigail rolled onto her side, both arms wrapped tight around the portrait. Abigail felt the portrait writhing against her chest as if a dozen snakes were escaping its canvas. She pulled it back from her body and looked down to see an unfamiliar image.

Lydia and Adeline were no longer seated in their usual spots on the canvas. In their place, Mallory and Cora sat tall and proud.

Confused and sure she'd grabbed a different portrait than the one she'd expected, Abigail inspected the edges of the familiar frame. There appeared to be layers of portraits bound to the backing. Prying at one edge in disbelief, Abigail peeled back the portrait of Mallory and Cora to reveal the portrait of Lydia and Adeline. Then, another layer—a portrait of Delilah, Constance, and Abigail.

"What the—"

Movement beside her caught her attention. Abigail quickly rolled to the side, expecting Shadow Mother to have approached in her bewilderment. Instead, she came face-to-face with Constance's charred, smoldering corpse.

Her sister's lips parted.

Her bloodshot eyes opened.

Then, something even more surprising happened.

Constance sat up.

CHAPTER 21

LYDIA

Lydia watched her daughter's fine hair tumble in the upwelling bathwater, her thin limbs punch and kick beneath the surface, her face, eyes wide and mouth open screaming for help but impossible to hear, obscured by the rippling water as the tub chewed her up.

No matter how much Lydia groped and grabbed, no matter how deep or how shallow, she couldn't feel Adeline's body beneath the water. Couldn't save her from drowning.

Couldn't end their hell.

Lydia screamed until the acrid taste of blood in her throat became an afterthought. She pulled her arms out of the tub, thinking she was somehow keeping Adeline from surfacing, then plunged in again to search, fruitlessly and endlessly.

How much time had passed? How long had she been there on her knees beside the tub, soaked through her nightgown, hyperventilating, and alone?

Seconds.

Minutes.

Hours.

Days.

Weeks.

An eternity.

As long as Adeline's open eyes and mouth called to her from beneath the water, Lydia would never quit. Time was irrelevant, a meaningless measurement of moments passed when no moments passed at all. They were trapped here in this hell, this eternal trauma.

"Wade!" Lydia cried out for her husband, unable to recall when she'd last seen him. He'd run into the room with her a lifetime ago before fleeing to find help.

In more desperate cries, Lydia called out for her mother. But she couldn't conjure her mother's face in her mind. She felt like she was summoning a stranger, someone she *should* call out for but had never seen. She'd somehow wiped the woman's face from her memory and replaced it with a shadow, a smear of death displacing a face once alive. The shadow felt familiar, like a danger she could easily spot but couldn't avoid, couldn't shed.

Lydia jumped as a booming voice overcame the sound of Adeline's tub thrashing echoing from the hard tile.

MOTHER

Hands shot out of the water—young, waterlogged, desperate hands. Adeline's manicured fingernails adorned each delicate finger.

Lydia grabbed the exposed forearms with such strength she feared she'd never release her grip again. She stood and yanked backward in one violent motion, leaving no effort untapped. She had *finally* found her daughter, and she would hold her forever.

The tub birthed Adeline to the bathroom, water pouring from her body to the floor and splashing the walls, sink, and toilet. Lydia's relieved cries came out as whimpers—shaky, uncontrolled exhalations of sound and emotion.

"Breathe, baby, *breathe!*"

Adeline gasped, eyes wide and mouth open exactly as they were under water but now drawing life from the air rather than death from the tub.

Lydia had her child in her arms again.

They collapsed in a shaking heap on the bathroom floor. And Lydia finally wept, crying deep sobs of immeasurable relief. She didn't care where Wade went or whether she'd ever see him again. The only person she'd ever truly loved—her child—was back in her arms, safe and recovering.

Lydia never saw the door open to the hall or heard the screams from her daughter's bedroom or from downstairs. Only when Adeline sat up and pointed to the open door did Lydia think of anything but her daughter.

Adeline blew water droplets from her lips and blinked wildly as she spoke for the first time since surfacing. "I know what to do. It's time, Mama."

"Time for what, baby?" Genuinely confused, Lydia didn't have a clue what Adeline meant.

"It's time to go home."

Adeline stood and pulled Lydia to her feet. Her strength seemed disproportionate to her tiny body. She laced her fingers into her mother's, flashed a smile, and stepped into the hall.

CHAPTER 22

MALLORY

Cora's dead body lay lifeless in the bed before Mallory. Seeing Cora that way, eyes closed and body immobile, ripped Mallory to pieces and cast her soul to the wind.

Cora was gone. She'd died in the cemetery embracing her baby.

Now, the baby lay in Mallory's arms, swaddled in a muddy cotton blanket.

She looked from the baby to the bed and realized for the hundredth time how much blood had stained Cora's clothes and bedsheets. She didn't understand how this kept happening. She'd cleaned Cora and the baby countless times.

Freshly washed clothes and sheets for Cora and a new blanket for the baby.

Then, after what seemed like only seconds, the stains returned, as if she'd never changed them. Mallory wondered if this was punishment for bringing Cora home. But what was she supposed to do? She couldn't bring herself to leave Cora out there.

But, she hadn't. Had she? No...

She'd found them secluded in the trees beside the graves of their kin. And she'd buried them. She remembered every mind-bending strike of the shovel as she dug their grave. The memory of placing Cora and the baby in the earth stood as clear as day at the front of her mind.

However, they were here, with her now. She had no recollection of unearthing them, hoisting them from the grave, bringing them back to the house using whatever strength remained in her pained body after a morning spent burying them.

Yet, here they were.

She looked into the upturned face of her granddaughter cradled in her arms. The baby's smooth, unblemished face stared back at her.

"She's asleep, that's all," Mallory said aloud. "They're just sleeping. They'll wake soon enough."

She knew that wasn't true but pinning down reality felt foolish at this point.

"You may not remember bringing them back here, but that doesn't change the fact that they're both..."

She couldn't bring herself to finish the sentence. Instead, she stood and placed the swaddled baby at the foot of the bed. She let her hand linger over the newborn for a few tentative seconds, just to be sure she wouldn't squirm in her blanket and roll off the bed.

Mallory stepped to Cora's closet and opened the rickety door her husband had haphazardly hung before his untimely death. For a skilled laborer, the man couldn't perform repairs in the house with any respectable level of proficiency. A stack of clean blankets and sheets filled the shallow closet from floor to ceiling. She'd pulled sheets and blankets from the stack all day but never put a dent in the pile. She did the same again and shut the door on its loose hinges with a heavy sigh.

Back at Cora's bedside, Mallory pulled back the blood-soaked sheets and let her heart break all over again. Cora's butchered, open wrists mocked her so she lay them across Cora's belly so she wouldn't have to see the wounds while she worked.

Without looking, she drew a washcloth from the bowl of water on the nightstand. As soon as she brought it to Cora's soiled face, she realized the cloth was as horribly soiled as Cora's nightgown. She squeezed her eyes shut and muttered a prayer.

"I can do all things through Christ which strengtheneth me."

When Mallory opened her eyes, the cloth appeared clean in her freshly scrubbed hand. She looked at the bowl of water on the nightstand, satisfied with its clear contents.

"Amen," she said with relief.

Mallory tended to her daughter's corpse, removing her iniquities, her grief, the macabre evidence of her death. She restored Cora, limb by limb, returning her to purity with every wipe of the cloth, kissing her hands and wrists before positioning them by her side on the new sheets.

She would repeat this sacrament for eternity if needed. She'd never let Cora down again. She'd vowed to honor her daughter in this way, and she intended to keep her word.

The baby swaddled at the foot of the bed whimpered, either hungry or displeased with her own unkempt state.

"Oh! Worry not my dear," Mallory said softly as she gently lifted the baby. "Grandma will clean you, too."

She set the baby beside her mother on the bed, trading coos and other baby noises as she worked the cloth about the infant's tiny body. Mallory glanced at Cora's face when the baby got a little too fussy, hopeful to witness a fluttering of her daughter's eyelids or a twitch of her mouth.

The tears would come then, when her hope peaked but her wishes remained unfilled. Still, she held on to the possibility that maybe, *just maybe*, Cora would eventually rouse at the sound of her baby's voice. If the cleansing could revive the daughter, perhaps it could revive the mother.

It didn't seem fair for Mallory to spend her foreseeable future alone, outside of these brief moments.

The heartache hit especially hard when she'd look down and realize the baby had slipped back to sleep. How she'd hoped to spend more time with her awake, telling stories about when Cora was a baby.

Mallory smiled through her tears thinking of Cora laying in her arms just like her granddaughter did then. "I'll do anything to get her back, Lord please."

She sent that prayer up for the hundredth time, then took her seat at the foot of the bed. She hesitated to look down at the baby's face, afraid she'd find her blanket filthy again, to restart the cycle. She'd stare at Cora instead, obsessing over the sweep of her upper lip, the gradual arc of her perfectly shaped nose. She'd stare and she'd pray until eventually, she'd slip into a depression so deep she couldn't fight off the crying.

She'd lose herself in her screams, quaking uncontrollably as her hands cupped the baby's sensitive ears. She squeezed her eyes shut as hard as she could for as long as she could, fearing—*knowing*—that when she did open them, the cycle would begin again.

But she could only hold out for so long. She had to open her eyes. And eventually, by a miracle of God, she opened them and found Cora staring back at her.

"Cora..."

Cora turned her head toward a pair of muffled voices in the hall outside their room.

One young and one older.

A child and her mother.

Cora sat up.

"It's time."

CHAPTER 23

DELILAH

Delilah floated above Constance's burned body in the sitting room. Her last memory was of sitting catatonic on the couch, screaming as she helplessly watched Constance burn. She couldn't rationalize time's passage since returning to the house, unable to run to Constance, to pound out the flames spreading across her child's body. The memory felt more like a dream than a lived experience.

Abigail had been there. Delilah had shielded her from the flames engulfing Constance and from the sight of her sister's demise. Abigail's heart had pounded in her tiny body as Delilah laid on her. The threat of losing both girls kept her pinned to Abigail, terrified to expose her youngest daughter while utterly heartbroken over seeing Constance ravaged by fire like a living sacrifice.

Was this all a repeated dream? She'd died without any of this happening; that, she was sure of. Perhaps she was a ghost, a guardian angel protecting Abigail but somehow not powerful enough to protect Constance.

None of it made sense to her.

Abigail burst into the room, but she looked different now. She was an adult. Delilah's memory slowly returned. She had seen Abigail as an adult when she and her sister had saved Delilah from this place and ferried her to the other side. She'd needed help because—

Shadow Mother had infected Delilah and clung to her like a poison cloud. Terror swelled in Delilah. Her loved ones had warned her not to come back here. Lydia and Constance had insisted she stay on the other side, in the afterlife. Apparently, she'd ignored their advice and returned to the home, but in some other form.

Below her, Abigail collapsed on the floor beside Constance's badly damaged body. In her hands, she held the family portrait from the mantelpiece.

Delilah tried to reach for Abigail, tried to call her name, but she had no hands, no voice. She was merely an observer. Movement on the floor caught her attention. Constance was sitting up! Abigail appeared equally surprised, her raised eyebrows drawing into peaks and her jaw dropping. Abigail held the portrait at arm's length and inspected its surface, her brow turning down in confusion. That's when Delilah recognized herself and her girls in the portrait.

Delilah felt herself pulled to the center of the room like smoke drawn into a fan. She collected like a mist in the narrow gap between her daughters. A scream from down the hall drew their attention.

"Do something, Connie." Abigail's voice waxed and waned with fear.

A shadow poured across the floorboards in the hall, preceding a thick billow of smoke that rolled through the archway and into the sitting room, obscuring any view of the house beyond them. A figure stepped forward from the cloud. "I see you there, Delilah. Rise and join your daughters. I want you to watch this."

Delilah felt her spirit come together, a scattered mist of disparate ghostly particles, suspended about the floor now coming together like metal shavings collected on a magnet.

Delilah materialized between her girls in her burial gown.

Shadow Mother had them trapped with no way to escape. The dark entity floated closer, a tightly bound cloud, now taking on a distinctly human form, the features of a woman Delilah could not place but felt connected to. Ragged black hair framed a beautifully elegant face donning brilliant, shining onyx eyes. Her lips parted to reveal a tongue and teeth that moved like shifting black sand.

"Last woman standing." Shadow Mother pointed to Abigail. "It's time to come home for good."

Delilah, Abigail, and Constance scrambled to their feet. Delilah stepped between her girls and the demon. Shadow Mother approached, gliding closer, an angel of death possessing arresting beauty, coasting on a toxic breeze.

"I won't let you hurt us any longer," Delilah said. The anger in her voice was unmistakable. She was a mother cornered by a predator. She had nothing to lose by fighting as hard as she could. Delilah wasn't sure *how* she'd fight a spirit, but she didn't have time to think. It was time to finish this. She'd already lost her life, her marriage, the opportunity to raise her girls. She'd lost everything that mattered when she'd died in the flames of her car accident.

Shadow Mother inched closer. Abigail raised the portrait, pulling it away from her mother's back and holding it out to their side like a shield. Shadow Mother stopped, her face contorting into a curious grin.

"Aren't they beautiful? My prized possessions."

"Stop this now. Leave us. Leave this house. This is your last warning." Delilah felt powerful beyond any strength she'd possessed in the physical world. The feeling was addictive, a supernatural adrenaline far surpassing its natural state.

Delilah felt Constance grow more rigid at her back, possibly experiencing the same otherworldly rush as her mother. Perhaps they'd be strong enough together to protect Abigail.

Suddenly, a baby cried out in the upstairs hall.

A woman screamed.

Feet pounded on the ceiling above them.

Shadow Mother turned midair and bolted from the sitting room in a black streak of rage.

Delilah grabbed Abigail and flew for the front door, desperate to get her out of the house, away from danger. This was her opportunity to save her daughter. Abigail cried out for her to stop as Constance screamed up at the ceiling.

"Run! She's coming!"

CHAPTER 24

LYDIA

An acrid haze filled the upstairs hall from smoke flowing in a steady stream up the stairs. Lydia recoiled at the stench as Adeline pulled her out of the illuminated bathroom and into the unlit hall. Exhausted from what felt like an endless fight for Adeline's life, Lydia's wrecked nerves obscured her thoughts and prevented her from processing the abnormal atmosphere. She shivered as water ran from her saturated clothes in frigid rivulets down her legs.

"We need to get out of here. Something's on fire down—"

Lydia stopped abruptly as she turned her attention to the open bedroom door across the hall. Beyond Adeline, a teenage girl, beautiful in her ghostly pallor, lay in her daughter's bed.

Fingers still intertwined with Lydia's, Adeline ran to the girl. Instinctively, Lydia grabbed her hand, but Adeline was too fast and easily slipped from her weak, wet grip. Lydia barely kept her balance when her feet slid on the hardwood floor as she reached for Adeline.

"Cora!" Adeline said excitedly.

"You know her?" Lydia's thoughts evaded her and her stomach coiled in knots when she saw Cora's butchered wrists. "My God, what—"

Coming fully into the doorway, Lydia saw a woman holding a baby stand from a chair in the corner. Lydia's breath caught in her throat. The haggard woman was oddly familiar. They had to be related. But Lydia had never met this woman, at least not that she could recall. The woman's face loosened as her teary eyes settled on Lydia, a look of confusion dawning on her swollen face.

"Who are you?" the woman asked.

Lydia opened her mouth to answer, but Cora asked Adeline a troubling question of her own. "How did we get here?"

"I'm not sure, but Constance and Abigail need us. Shadow Mother—"

The haggard woman let out a horrified whimper as her knees buckled. Luckily, the chair caught her, otherwise,

Lydia feared the woman would have collapsed to the floor and dropped the baby.

"Bring her to me!" Cora said, wincing as she stretched her damaged arms for the baby.

"Who are these people, Adeline?" Lydia stepped in the woman's direction, eager to scoop the baby from her hands before she dropped it, but Adeline pushed past her and beelined for the woman.

"Adeline!" The girl's erratic behavior shocked Lydia.

"This is Cora, and her mother, Mallory. Trust me," Adeline insisted as she snatched the infant from the woman's loose grip.

"Bring her here!" Cora yelled, her words slurred and mushy.

Adeline lowered the baby in her arms and shoved past Lydia, away from the bed. Lydia reeled, utterly perplexed by Adeline's actions.

"What are you doing?"

Adeline ran for the door, the baby crying in her arms.

Cora spilled from the bed in a tangle of sheets as she reached for the infant, desperate to pull her from Adeline.

"I'm sorry, but this is the only way!" Adeline yelled without looking back.

Lydia ran after her.

Crossing the hall, Adeline pivoted into the bathroom.

"No, Adeline!" Lydia screamed, unable to reach the doorway before her daughter and the baby reached the tub. Lydia slipped on a standing puddle, crashed into the bathroom door frame, and fell hard to the floor. The hall spun in her dazed vision.

"Bring her back!" Mallory cried as she stumbled into the hall and slipped on the wet floor beside Lydia. Seconds ago, she'd seemed on the verge of a blackout. As she struggled to her feet, Lydia saw Cora crawling across the floor behind them.

In the bathroom, Adeline turned and held the crying baby over the churning tub. "She's the only one who hasn't crossed over. She's the only spirit Shadow Mother has full possession of. Not anymore."

"Don't—" Lydia's words fell away as Adeline pulled the baby tight to her chest and pitched forward into the tub.

Lydia reached the tub first. As she plunged her arms and head into the water, Adeline's hand shot from the water and ripped her from her feet into a black abyss. Hands clawed at her legs as she went limp in the rip current.

A second body plunged into the flow beside her.

Then another.

Lydia immediately felt an inexplicable tension, an unseen looming danger, waiting for them somewhere in their midst. She rolled in the dark ocean of shadows, trying to find her bearings in the tumultuous flow. Finally, she spotted Adeline's silhouette ahead of her in the flow, beyond her reach, her hair suspended in the current, her face turned to the vast emptiness ahead.

Lydia let go and trusted Adeline as the violent current swept them into the bleak expanse between the living and the dead.

CHAPTER 25

CONSTANCE

Incapacitated by fear and indecision, Constance watched her mother shove Abigail into the foyer and toward the front door.

Run after them. Leave and never come back, she thought.

She'd wanted none of this. It seemed like a millennium since she'd argued with Abigail about this house, pleading with her to stay away. She swore it'd kill her sister, and it nearly had. Twice. This opportunity felt too good to be true, a last chance to flee and leave it all behind.

Constance stumbled into the foyer as her mother disappeared through the open front doorway with Abigail.

Run! Go now!

For a moment, she thought Shadow Mother would double back, stalk her mother and sister down, and finish them before they could escape.

She looked to her right, toward the stairs, toward the screams echoing off the walls upstairs. Shadow Mother had already reached the stairs, a putrid tail of smoke and ash trailing behind her as she climbed.

Constance realized they'd never escape their demon. That evil had followed them in their dreams. It had hurt Abigail in Aunt Jenny's home the moment their defenses had collapsed. It had influenced other dead spirits in their path. They couldn't outrun the beast hunting them. Shadow Mother wouldn't stop until she had Abigail.

Someone crashed onto the floor above her again, the violent sound pulling her back from the edge of inaction.

Constance ran.

As she gained on Shadow Mother, the taste of charred wood and burnt atmosphere filled her open mouth and cinched her throat tight. She didn't care. She was a ghost, the physical threats of her previous life could no longer harm her.

Behind Constance in the foyer, the front door slammed shut.

Take her far from here, Mama. I need to see this through. I need to make sure she never gets to Abigail again, even if it means I must endure an eternity chasing a nightmare.

"Constance! Stop!"

Damn it! Mama was close. She sounded like she was right behind her. Constance had banked on Mama staying with Abigail. She feared looking away from Shadow Mother would slow her down, so she kept her eyes forward and flew up the stairs. Halfway up, she heard bodies slamming into the tub. One, then another, and another.

Shadow Mother let loose a wretched, guttural scream. Whatever was happening in the bathroom, it had clearly upset the beast.

"Please, Connie! Stop!" Mama had gained on her.

"I must do this! We can't run forever!"

A few steps ahead of her, Shadow Mother disappeared through the bathroom doorway, her alien screams filling the air like tortured, twisting steel.

Constance couldn't believe what happened next. Shadow Mother dove into the tub, breaking through the barrier between worlds like a semi-truck plowing into an Olympic pool.

Now on the landing at the top of the stairs, Constance saw twisted bedsheets stretched from Abi's room into the hall, soaked through with water. A baby's blanket lay discarded beside the bed in the chaos.

Constance understood.

The screams.

The puddles everywhere.

The crashing footfalls.

They'd all escaped through the tub.

And Shadow Mother had gone in after them.

Constance drew a deep breath and sprinted into the bathroom.

"Connie! Don't—"

Constance left her mother's pleading voice behind as she plunged into the tub. A cool vein of rushing water seized her immediately. Her senses heightened, and her vision adjusted to the sudden change of light. Behind her, Mama crashed through the rays of light streaming in from the bathroom above. Mama's flailing hands found her in the twilight darkness and pulled her close as the flow drew them further into the deep.

Constance spun around as they accelerated in the flow and spotted Shadow Mother, her dark form billowing in the current like a black sheet in a hurricane. They had to catch up with her before she overtook the others.

Feeling tremendous guilt, Constance pushed off her mother. Delilah's eyes widened as she realized her daughter's intentions. Constance broke eye contact, pressed her body into a narrow profile, and rocketed into the current.

CHAPTER 26

ADELINE

An underwater forest rolled beneath Adeline as the flow shuffled them toward the afterlife. Clara, swaddled in a tight bundle against her chest, squirmed and wriggled. Adeline thought the poor infant must be terrified by their haphazard plunge into the flow. But terror was justified if it led to survival, and Adeline had rolled the dice when she'd assumed this was the best way to free Clara from the Whispering House and get an advantage over Shadow Mother. Clearly, they stood little chance in the house. Shadow Mother was far too powerful there.

Back in the horrors of the house, she'd realized Clara hadn't crossed over. She suspected that when Clara reached the afterlife, Shadow Mother could no longer possess her. She also hoped to provide a distraction for the others. Hopefully, they'd sought shelter and helped Abigail escape the house while Shadow Mother pursued her.

Of course, the success of her plan relied on her ability to evade Shadow Mother in the flow. Adeline should have an advantage in the lightless portal she'd traveled in nearly every night for the past twenty years. She'd never encountered dangers in her travels. Now, she was in a race to reach the other side and to liberate Clara before Shadow Mother could snatch her back to the Whispering House.

A hand emerged from the darkness and grabbed Adeline's ankle. Surprised, she cried out as she lost momentum. She kicked vigorously, nearly losing her grip on Clara as her body whipped and bucked, too terrified to look down. Ahead, Adeline saw a column of radiant light pouring into the flow from the afterlife.

She was almost there. Adeline couldn't lose like this. She refused to fail this close to the end.

The hands climbed up her legs, forcing her to look down into the face of her attacker.

"Mama!"

Lydia climbed her body as they blasted through the current, soon coming face-to-face with Adeline as Clara squirmed between them. Adeline felt tremendous relief that her mother was the one who'd found her, but she immediately recognized the danger of slowing. Shadow

Mother had to be close behind them in the darkness. They couldn't afford to slow their escape.

Adeline looked down between her feet into the abyss and saw a broad swath of shadow quickly moving toward them. That had to be Shadow Mother, and she was moving much too fast for Adeline's liking.

Adeline saw Lydia staring down at Shadow Mother, realizing their danger, her eyes enlarged by fear.

Lydia pulled her gaze back to Adeline, grabbed her daughter's shoulders and mouthed the words *I love you* before shoving Adeline and Clara hard toward the light closing on them from above.

"Mama!" Adeline's exclamation disintegrated into garbled aquatic blither in the liquid between them. "Pull her into the light!"

Lydia's face brightened when she seemingly understood Adeline's plan.

The distance grew between them as Adeline sped up, no longer slowed by her mother. Adeline squinted as the water brightened around them in a flash. Turbulence jostled Adeline and Clara as they reached the end of the flow, the place where they'd either succeed or fail in her plan.

Blinded by the intense illumination, Adeline lost sight of her mother. She placed a hand on the crown of Clara's head and said a quick prayer. Suddenly, she doubted whether her plan would work. She questioned whether her mother would survive an encounter with Shadow Mother in the flow.

It was too late for doubt. She had to have faith.

As she surfaced, she raised Clara above her head, drew a deep breath, and screamed for Aunt Jenny and the rest of their family.

CHAPTER 27

CONSTANCE

Shadow Mother's undulating darkness intermittently obscured the light filtering through the water ahead of Constance and Delilah. The light streamed to them from the other side, an indicator that their journey would end soon. Constance was quickly closing the gap between them and Shadow Mother. As she neared confrontation with the entity who'd ended her life and destroyed her family, an irrepressible rage built in her.

Beyond Shadow Mother's hypnotic flowing form, a body spun and slowed in the current. But Constance couldn't see which of the other women it could be. Adeline, Lydia, Cora, and Mallory had entered the flow before her; it could be any of them.

A sudden shift in the pattern of layered darkness startled her. Shadow Mother appeared to be flailing, struck by something substantial. Anxious excitement flitted in her gut and spread into her shaking limbs. Facing the decision of slowing her flight to approach cautiously or diving headfirst into the action, Constance chose the latter. She couldn't afford to forfeit the element of surprise or the force her speed would provide on impact.

Behind her, Delilah struggled to catch up, soaring awkwardly in the eddies and currents. Constance wanted to spare her mother from the fight, unsure whether she'd survive or evade serious injury. Delilah wasn't built for revenge. But Constance couldn't control how this confrontation would unfold once it started, and she might need help.

Roughly fifty yards ahead now, Shadow Mother sailed erratically toward the light. With only another minute until they'd meet in the flow, Constance prepared her heart for battle. Looking down, she watched the vast underwater forest passing below them, treetops swaying as their group's wake disturbed the calm below. Constance imagined she was soaring over the trees surrounding their home. She envisioned their cemetery path winding between the Whispering House and their family, guiding them like the squiggly lines on a roadmap.

That cemetery was full of bodies because of the cursed creature tumbling ahead of her.

Constance looked up from the ocean floor and realized she was about to collide with Shadow Mother. Without warning, the entity had considerably slowed. Constance didn't have time to adjust. She tensed her muscles, extended her arms, and prepared for impact.

Their waterborne bodies met with violent force. Disoriented by the sudden change of speed and enveloped in a sheet of blinding darkness, Constance punched and kicked with all her strength, landing blows on a body she couldn't see. She felt Shadow Mother's firm muscles and hard bones beneath her strikes. Blow after blow, her rage compounded, eventually boiling over. This was her nightmare. From an early age, Constance had terrifying dreams of fighting underwater. Now, her frustration compounded as, like in her dreams, her blows had no effect. She couldn't win, couldn't break the will of her opponent. This was that nightmare, manifesting now as reality.

A set of hands wrapped around her body and pulled her backward. She assumed Delilah had finally joined her, but she couldn't confirm who it was as she fought deep in Shadow Mother's surrounding darkness. The hands separated her from Shadow Mother. She finally saw the others. Lydia and Shadow Mother spun, tangled in a slow, agonizing wrestling match. Beyond them, about to exit the flow into the afterlife, Mallory and Cora swam into the column of light, reaching for a pair of hands penetrating the surface.

Delilah released Constance and swung gracefully in the current until she landed a raised knee in Shadow Mother's back.

They swarmed the demon.

Joining her mother and Lydia in the fight gave Constance permission to release every pent-up frustration, every horrible memory, every ounce of vengeful spite she'd allowed to fester over the past twenty years since her horrible death. She didn't deserve the death dealt to her. Her family didn't deserve the haunting they'd endured for a century at the hands of this hateful devil. And now they had their opportunity to fight back.

To pummel.

To gnash and gouge and claw and kick.

They'd tear Mother apart in the flow.

Each of them screaming, cursing, raging—killing.

Constance wanted to kill. She craved death at her hand. Blood on her tongue. An eye for an eye.

For her and her Mama.

For Cora, Mallory, and baby Clara.

For Lydia and Adeline.

She wanted justice.

In the mayhem and growing light, Delilah swept Constance in her arms and squeezed her into Shadow Mother's back. From the front of the fight, Lydia's hands gripped her arms and pulled tight, fully wrapping Shadow Mother between them. They'd formed a tight mass around Mother as the light intensified. She writhed and screamed in their grip, fighting to escape them, to avoid the light.

When they breached the surface, Constance lost herself in the screams of her loved ones.

They'd reached their point of redemption.

Their resolution had finally come.

CHAPTER 28

CONSTANCE

The women of the Whispering House opened their eyes to the tranquil, sunlit cemetery. They sat in a line, hands joined, bearing no physical evidence of their struggle with Shadow Mother in the space between life and death.

Before them, lay an open grave.

Constance drew a deep, centering breath and exhaled with relief, her nose and lungs filling with the scent of dewy grass and pine. The cool morning breeze carried the smell of jasmine and recently disturbed clay. She took stock of the faces at her sides. Delilah sat on her left, Lydia and Adeline on her right.

Movement drew Constance's attention to the edge of the cemetery where she watched Cora ease herself up from the forest floor. Blinking and wiping stray hairs from her face with one hand, Cora sat up, cradling Clara to her chest. Cora looked down into her daughter's face with joyous tears slipping down her cheeks. They'd finally crossed over, mother and child, reunited in death and eternal love. Cora stood and made her way into the clearing, spotted Constance, and walked in their direction.

"It worked!" Adeline's excited voice broke the silence.

Constance turned to her young cousin and smiled. "You are something else, kid."

"Amen to that," Lydia said as she hugged Adeline with one arm.

"Mother?" A shaky, distressed voice escaped the open grave. Constance exchanged a shocked look with the others before they leaned forward to see Mallory kneeling at one end of the grave and a confused, confused woman kneeling at the other.

"Mother!" Mallory's quivering hands shot to her mouth. The woman at the other end of the grave pressed her hands into the red clay walls, her dazed eyes fixed on Mallory.

Perfectly statuesque as she leaned in closer, Constance watched in awe, afraid to disturb the scene playing out below her. At her side, Delilah quickly stood to intercept Cora and Clara who approached from a few yards away.

Delilah whispered something to Cora before guiding her and Clara to the grass beside them.

In the grave, a mother and daughter reunited, finally unbound by the afterlife.

"Mother, it's me. It's Mallory."

Mallory's mother steadied her breathing and pulled her hands from the clay walls. She leaned forward onto her hands to inspect Mallory's face as if she didn't believe her eyes.

"I...I see you. But..." The woman's lip quivered with emotion. "Is this real? Am I dreaming?"

"No, Mother." Mallory slowly crawled to her mother, stopping only a foot or so from her face. "We're dead."

Mother's quivering lip steadied and her eyes searched Mallory's face for evidence of betrayal, seemingly unsure if she could trust what she saw and heard.

Mallory lifted her mother's hand in hers and pressed it to her face. Her mother's fingers streaked moist clay onto Mallory's cheek. "I'm right here. You're not dreaming. We're *here*."

Mother looked up at the faces framing the grave's opening. Constance's heart throbbed with sympathy for the pain and confusion she saw in the face staring up at her.

"Grace. Your name is Grace. You were born and raised in James City County, Virginia. You ..." Mallory looked away for a moment to gather herself and blink back her tears. "You got sick. You couldn't stay with us anymore. I was little."

"I went to the hospital," Grace said, her voice slightly distant as she recalled her life.

Mallory cried softly and squeezed Grace's hand tighter to her face.

"Yes, you did. And you stayed there."

Grace's face darkened as her memories returned.

"I died there."

"Yes, you did." Mallory said, hitching her breath.

Grace's eyebrows narrowed and her face screwed into a troubled knot as she looked deeper into Mallory's face.

"And your father left me there." Grace leaned forward. "He *buried* me there?"

Mallory nodded slowly. "Yes. He did."

Grace looked up at her descendants crowded around the grave, a weary gaggle of curious onlookers. Though they'd done nothing wrong, Constance felt like a deer in a hunter's rifle sight as Grace's eyes flitted between their faces. Constance realized Cora had handed Clara to Delilah.

Surprised, she watched Cora climb into the grave before holding her open hands up to Delilah.

"Hand her to me. It's okay."

Delilah hesitated for a second, then handed Clara down to Cora. Constance considered how odd it was to see someone hand a baby to someone standing in a grave.

Never the twain shall meet, Constance thought.

"And this is Cora, your granddaughter," Mallory said as Cora kneeled beside her mother, angling Clara for Grace to see her face.

"I remember now." The words slipped from Grace's mouth in a pleasant whisper. Her face uncoiled and her eyes lightened. "I remember her–but only after I'd passed. I couldn't leave you and come here. I wasn't ready. But then, something happened to me. It was hell. Oh, Mallory. I'm so–" Grace buried her face in her hands and gave herself over to understanding.

"No. Never apologize. You did nothing wrong. That wasn't you. You did the best you could."

Mallory and Grace slowly unraveled into each other's arms, tears flowing freely as Cora laid her head on her mother's back and cried with them.

One after another, the women of the Whispering House climbed into Grace's grave. All except Constance, who stood above them, fighting to accept that Grace no longer fell under the possession of the demon who'd haunted them for so many precious, wasted years until they'd shed it like necrotic flesh in their transition to the afterlife, cast into the vast dark purgatory between life and death.

So much pain. So much loss.

Constance blinked away frustrated tears and looked up at the swaying trees. A tsunami of emotions threatened to break over her. To pound her into oblivion. She'd died so young. Her mother had died so violently. And Abigail had spent the past twenty years in mourning, living a lie, and running for her life.

Lydia—my God, she'd buried herself with Adeline.

A murmuration of starlings appeared from above the trees, shifting in columns and rows, a tight formation of black bodies against the bright sky. Their shapes morphed and flattened before expanding into explosive movements.

"Connie."

Constance looked down at her mother standing in the grave at her feet. The other women held each other in a tight group, sharing in the relief of Grace and Mallory's homecoming.

Delilah held her hand up, beckoning Constance into the grave.

"Come on, baby. Join us."

Approaching voices on the cemetery path. Aunt Jenny, Uncle Hank, Uncle Wade, and several other family members jogged down the path to greet them.

All this joy and all Constance felt was–*grief*.

"I can't."

Constance turned from her mother, away from the women in the grave and her family, and walked down the path to the Whispering House.

She needed to go home.

She needed Abigail.

CHAPTER 29

ABIGAIL

Abigail struggled through the front door of the bookstore, carrying a hefty cardboard box of newly delivered books threatening to break loose from her hand. She lifted her knee and pinned the box against the doorframe, accidentally dropping her keys between her feet.

"Yo! Connie! Can I get a hand!"

"On my way!" Constance called from the back office. She popped into view a second later, an unlit cigarette tucked behind one ear.

"Busted! You told me you quit!" Abigail yelled.

"What? Oh, shit." Constance snatched the cigarette from her ear and accidentally dropped it on the floor.

"I saw that. Why do you think I said something? You can grab it in a minute, just help me before I drop this box and eat the cost of more damaged books I can't return."

Constance grabbed the box from her sister's shaking arms just in time. Stretching her arms, Abigail flexed her stiff, aching fingers. She grimaced as the cool winter breeze blew a handful of crisp leaves into the foyer before the door closed.

"Great. One more thing to clean." Abigail peeled her puffy, tan down-filled winter coat off as she crossed the store to the long checkout counter along the far wall. "The heat in here feels amazing."

"I'm glad you like it. I can't remember what it feels like," Constance said flatly.

"Oh, stop being so dramatic. I swear." Abigail searched blindly with one hand under the counter for a box cutter.

"Looking for this?" Constance held the red box cutter up, waving it back and forth to tease Abigail.

"Yes." Abigail tried to grab the box cutter, but Constance pulled it out of reach and slid it across the counter in the opposite direction.

"Oops."

"Connie!"

Constance laughed and snatched her stray cigarette from the carpet while Abigail walked to the far end of the counter and grabbed the box cutter before it fell from the edge.

"We're in our thirties. When will you grow up and stop picking on me?" Abigail asked.

"Literally never. Knowing that there's an afterlife, I can confidently say I'll *never* stop."

They both laughed the kind of healthy laugh only close siblings understand.

"Good one. I gotta give it to you. You've kept your sense of humor despite having all the reasons in the world *not* to."

"Thanks," Constance said.

"How's the story coming along?" Abigail pulled the box cutter's blade across the taped center of the package while being careful not to press the blade too far into the box and damage an exposed book cover. She'd made that mistake too many times.

"I'm nearly done with edits. And I think I've got the perfect title," Constance outlined an imaginary marquee in the air between them. "*Banish the Dead.* What do you think?"

Abigail grinned. "I love it."

"Mean it?"

"Yeah, I really do. It's fitting, considering how weird and dark our story is. It's not every day an author gets to tell a story about sending their cursed loved ones to the other side."

"Thanks! So, where'd you go before the post office? It seemed like you were gone forever."

"I stopped to grab a little something special for everyone." Abigail pulled the top flaps of the box open and pulled packing paper away from the books. "Sweet! Our restock order of *The Talisman* came in. Oh, and *The Haunting of Hill House*, too."

"Don't change the subject. You know I'm going to badger you about what you picked up. Is it edible? Is it chocolate, round, and rhymes with 'fake'?" Constance sighed and pretended to dream about chocolate cake.

"Not quite. You'll have to wait until we get home to find out. That's why I called it a surprise, dummy."

Constance tilted her head to one side, leaned on the counter, and squinted like a suspicious detective. "What are you plotting, lady?"

"Like I said, it's a surprise. Now stop asking me or I'll start asking questions about that nasty cigarette you scooped from the floor."

Abigail placed the packing sheet on the countertop, hoisted an armful of books from the box, and crossed the shop to a sparsely stocked shelf below a handwritten sign that read, *Horror (The Good Stuff)*. Abigail had always loved thrillers and horror stories, and she took pride in having the largest horror selection of any bookstore in the area, maybe the state.

"As soon as I stock this box, I'll be ready to roll out."

"So early? Aren't you always obsessing over staying open longer so we can squeeze another five dollars of sales out of the day?"

"Like I said, I want to get home early for the surprise. Please set that packing sheet next to the computer when you go back to the office. I'll update the inventory in the morning."

"Wow, waiting until the morning to update inventory? Who is this devilishly rebellious woman? What have you done with my sister?" Constance grabbed the sheet from the counter and disappeared into the office.

Abigail rolled her eyes and smiled as she returned to the counter for another armful of books and anxiously checked the clock behind the counter. As the second hand rolled upward and finally crossed the twelve, the bell over the door rang.

Right on cue, Mrs. Harting stepped through the door, pulling the collars of her tan coat to her neck to fend off the frigid wind. As she'd done a thousand times before, Abigail put on her best smile.

"Good morning, Mrs. Harting. Looking for a particular book today?"

"Good morning, dear. No, thank you. I'm just looking around," Mrs. Harting replied in her usual fashion.

"Of course. Let me know if I can help you with anything."

Abigail looked back over her shoulder at the office where Constance was gathering her things in anticipation of their drive home. They exchanged a simple, knowing smile, a gentle and affectionate exchange, a silent acknowledgement of their shared experience. This was their routine, mundane life together, and they'd never take it for granted again.

After perusing the thriller titles and stopping briefly to examine the bare-chested studs dominating the covers of a few romance paperbacks, Mrs. Harting made her way to the horror section.

"This one always gets me," she said, tapping the spine of *The Haunting of Hill House* with one crooked, arthritic finger. "There's something odd about it that makes me feel like I've been in that place."

"That makes perfect sense," Abigail replied.

A few moments later, Mrs. Harting completed her round of the store and made her way to the door.

"Enjoy the rest of your day, Mrs. Harting," Abigail said, setting the box and packing materials on the floor behind the counter.

"Please do the same, dear. Tell your beautiful family I said 'hello'."

Abigail walked to the door as Mrs. Harting slipped into the brisk late winter breeze and crossed the parking lot on foot.

"I wonder if she'll ever find her way home," Constance said as she approached from the office.

Abigail flipped the *Open!* sign hanging in the window beside the door to *Closed* and took her coat from Constance.

"I'll miss her when she does," Abigail said.

Abigail tossed her keys into the wicker basket on the kitchen counter and flipped the overhead light on.

"God, I hate that light. It's so damn bright," Constance said as she set two large paper grocery bags on the kitchen counter beside the sink.

"Never change, Connie. I don't know what I'd do if you weren't complaining about something." Abigail smiled to show she was joking.

"I know what you could do," Constance replied.

"You'd better get those comments out of your system now before everyone comes over, or you're gonna get an earful from Mama."

"So true. Speaking of, are you ready now or do you need to dust and sweep one more time so Mama doesn't find out you live like a slob?"

Abigail laughed, her heart swelling with love for Constance. She was all Abigail ever needed in life. Abigail would probably never marry or have kids, and that was fine with her. She loved the life they'd built together. They had peace. They had each other.

"Let's do this. I'll be ready by the time you get back." Abigail walked down the short hall to the stairs leading to the second floor. Pausing with one foot on the bottom step, she held one hand out in an exaggerated arc, like a game show assistant revealing what hid behind door number one. "After you, ma'am."

"If I must," Constance grumbled and stepped past Abigail. As she climbed the steps behind her sister, Abigail grinned at the thought of how different the house would look and feel soon.

Reaching the landing at the top of the stairs, Constance walked into the bathroom and turned around with her hand on the doorknob. Abigail's stomach tumbled thinking of the darkness in the bathroom behind her sister. She wasn't sure if she'd ever be able to reign her imagination in after all she'd seen in that room over her years.

"I'll be right back. Arm yourself while I'm gone. They're going to be annoyingly helpful, and you know it. Love you." Constance grinned and closed the door before Abigail could reply.

Abigail leaned her forehead on the closed door and allowed her imagination to pull her apart like a quartered criminal tied to four horses. She closed her eyes and listened as her sister filled the tub. Abigail hated when Constance traveled to the other side. But it was necessary. It was the price they paid for Constance to remain with her and remain aware of where she belonged. Staying with the living for too long presented hazards. They could bend their reality, cheat life and death, but they couldn't completely disregard nature. Nature had a way of winning.

No matter how many times Constance and the others had traveled the flow, Abigail worried something would eventually go wrong, a statistical inevitability threatening to upend her life again. She feared an expected change in the portal would prevent Constance from returning. She worried about the dangers in the unexplored abyss surrounding the flow.

Most of all, Abigail worried Constance would return with a longer shadow.

Abigail whispered a prayer for Constance. "Please be safe. Come back as you left. I love you."

She turned from the door, crossed the hall, and entered her bedroom. She closed her bedroom door to create another barrier between her and the sound of the water filling the tub. The early afternoon sun penetrated the sheer curtain, casting a pink hue on the walls, dresser, and ceiling.

"She'll be fine. Stop getting worked up over something that hasn't happened," she told herself. She chose to think positive thoughts of their pending reunion to distract herself. In a few hours, she'd sit on the bed with Adeline and Cora, and they'd share fun stories about the games they'd played and how they'd hid from their parents when it was time to do chores. Innocent, inconsequential memories. The stuff childhoods are made of.

Downstairs, their mothers would cook and clean and tell stories of their own. Voices would fill the normally quiet house, mingling with the comforting smell of their recent dinner. They'd spend the night sipping lukewarm tea at the kitchen table where they'd tell more stories, tales they'd told a hundred times over, of their favorite memories together in the house. And they'd laugh at each story as if it was the first time it'd been told.

Abigail's worry slowly shifted to anticipation. Her family was coming to visit. And she had a special afternoon planned.

Abigail surveyed the room, lightly outfitted with the belongings of several young girls. Adeline's stuffed animals lay in a haphazard pile in the large basket beside the dresser. Cora's stuffed dolls sat on the dresser top beside Abigail's row of books.

The sound of water filling the tub stopped.

Abigail laid down and pulled a pillow over her ears, staring at the pink shades dancing across the wall as her sister drowned in the tub across the hall.

Come back as you left.

CHAPTER 30

ABIGAIL

The portrait of Aunt Lydia and Adeline sat in its rightful place on the fireplace mantel in the sitting room. Alone for the moment, Abigail stood in the center of the room, enjoying the sounds of her mother and Aunt Lydia working in the kitchen. She'd dedicated every spare minute of free time and every dollar of profit from the bookstore to renovating the parts of the house needing the most attention–starting with the new floorboards beneath her feet. Eli had been kind enough to lend his talents to the job, insisting on replacing the sitting room floors himself. Abigail couldn't watch him remove the old charred, stained floorboards. Her emotions got the best of her. Apparently, his emotions got the best of him as well. Abigail heard him sniffling and quietly crying as he pulled the boards up one at a time and carried them from the house to his truck. She never discussed the past with Eli, but she suspected he'd gained as much closure from the job as she did.

"They look great, dear."

Abigail turned and found Delilah leaning against the archway, drying her hands on a dishtowel.

"Thanks. It needed to be done. I think Eli did a bang-up job."

"He really did. We're almost ready for dinner. Can you grab the others from the yard for me?"

"Of course." Abigail followed her mother to the kitchen, peeking up the stairs as they went. From her vantage point downstairs, she saw only the top third of the dark bathroom doorway. No sounds, no movement—everything seemed safe.

They entered the kitchen to the sounds of plates being stacked on the counter and the comforting smell of buttered food cooking. Lydia and Delilah were nearly done preparing a large meal for the family, complete with baked chicken, mashed potatoes and gravy, butter beans, and freshly baked rolls. The intoxicating smells threw Abigail's stomach into a fit.

"That smells amazing." Abigail stepped to the back door, lingering for just a moment to enjoy the smells.

"Well, there's plenty here, so bring your appetite to the table with ya," Lydia said.

Abigail opened the back door and found Aunt Jenny, Uncle Hank, and Uncle Wade sitting on the screened-in porch.

"Hey, look who showed up! Where ya been hidin' girl?" Aunt Jenny was all smiles despite the ribbing.

"Sorry, I was checking out some of the work Eli did in the sitting room and making a list for the next project." She tapped the side of her head with her pointer finger. "Dinner's almost ready."

"Oh! I guess I need to get up and set the table then. Excuse me, fellas." Aunt Jenny stood and crossed the porch, relieving Abigail of her position at the door.

Abigail leaned out onto the back deck. To her right, Mallory and Cora tended to their garden. They couldn't visit without spending time out there, working the vegetables and pulling weeds. Abigail was grateful they enjoyed cooking so Abigail didn't have to. To her left, Adeline danced erratically in the yard. After a few seconds of observation, Abigail realized Adeline was playing a game with several starlings swooping down from the trees to the yard and back. Her long curls bounced along her shoulders and the back of her dress as she spun and sprinted about the grass to dodge the incoming birds.

"Dinner!" Abigail called.

"Okay!" Mallory replied. She set her garden tools in a bucket and handed it to Cora before they stood and crossed the yard to the house.

"I'll be there in a minute. Can we come back out after dinner?" Adeline said.

"Yes, but not to play. I have a surprise for everyone." Abigail retreated to the house before Adeline could inquire further about her plans. Stepping back into the house, Abigail joined Aunt Jenny and Constance to finish setting the table. Looking over the partially set table as her family buzzed with conversation and laughter, Abigail realized how special moments with family were. She had these souls together for only a brief time. She'd taken them for granted when they were there in the flesh. She wouldn't make that mistake again.

"Everything good?" Constance asked, setting the last place at the table.

"Everything's great," Abigail said. And she truly meant it. She'd never had more love in her life than she did when she was the only living soul in the room.

"Well, that was amazing. Thank you for cooking, ladies." Uncle Wade leaned back in his chair and rubbed his belly with one hand.

"I hope you saved room for dessert. We've got pound cake and fresh fruit over here." Aunt Lydia said without looking up from the kitchen sink.

"Leave those, Aunt Lydia. We'll take care of the dishes after we get back."

"Can we take care of dessert after we get back, too?" Constance asked.

"That's not a bad idea. We can do whatever it is you've got planned before dessert, Abigail," Delilah said. "That'll give us some time to let our stomachs settle."

"I second that motion," Aunt Jenny said.

"Okay. Would you ladies care to join me in the yard? Sorry, gentlemen. This is an exclusive invite." Abigail pushed back from the table, and the others followed her lead.

"No problem whatsoever. I promise that pound cake will be here when you ladies are done," Uncle Hank said.

"You'd better not touch that cake before we get back. Do you hear me?" Aunt Jenny poked him in the ribs.

"Yes ma'am."

Without another word, the women of the Whispering House followed Abigail from the house to the backyard. She guided them to the center of the grass and stopped.

"Would you ladies join me?" Abigail extended her hands to her sister and mother. Lydia, Adeline, Mallory, and Cora joined them to complete the circle.

"What's this all about, Abi?" Delilah asked.

"Well, Constance and I have been busy working on the house while you've all been away, and we wanted to show you one last thing we've done. We love each of you so very much and we've finally righted some long overdue wrongs." Abigail smiled to lighten the mood and show the others her excitement.

"Well, let's get on with it then," Adeline said. The rest of the group broke into laughter.

"Very well, then. This way, please."

Abigail led them down the cemetery path. No one spoke as they went, allowing the silence to amplify the mood. This time, the forest bordering the path remained dormant and tame. No spirits flitted about the trees. No voices emanated from the depths of the woods. At one point, Abigail worried that if she looked back, she'd find herself alone on the path. If that happened, she'd continue on and finish the job as she'd intended, confident that wherever the other women were at that moment, they'd know what she'd done to honor them. They'd know she'd finally set things right. Thankfully, they remained with her and the group reached the cemetery together.

"Oh my! Abigail!" Delilah spoke first. She went directly to Constance's grave to admire the newly installed headstone, which Abigail had previously hidden in the shed. A single red rose sat atop the stone. Abigail lifted it and handed it to Constance.

"So, *that's* where you went today. You went to the florist. Very nice, Abi," Constance said.

"Thanks. You know I'm not good at making special occasions special." Abigail held her hand out to show several other new headstones installed in a row beside Constance's. "I had one made for each of us. Cora, this one is yours and Clara's. I figured you'd prefer to stay together." Abigail lifted two roses from the headstone and handed them to Cora, who quickly took them before hugging Abigail so tight she thought she'd pop.

"Thank you, Abigail. I can't tell you how much this means to us. It's been so long." Cora couldn't finish. Her eyes filled with tears.

"And I placed you and Grace beside them," Abigail said as she took roses from the two stones and handed them to Mallory.

"Wait. Mother was buried in the Eastern State Hospital cemetery," Mallory said.

"She's here with us now. Where she belongs. Beside you, Cora, and Clara."

"You had her moved? Abigail. Constance. This is too much. I'm so overwhelmed." Mallory's tears came.

"She's home now. Where she belongs," Constance said, stepping close to Abigail.

"I wish she was here to see this," Mallory said, pressing her hand to her mouth.

"It's okay," Abigail said. "I understand it wasn't safe to let her into the flow. And she's watching Clara so that's a win."

"What's going on here, Abi?" Delilah's brow furrowed as she pointed to the headstone beside Constance's.

"I went ahead and set my plot while I was at it. There's no one to make sure I'm with you guys when my day finally comes, so I took care of it now."

"Yeah. But most people don't install their own headstone. That's a bit much, Abi," Delilah said.

Constance laughed. "You should have seen the staff at Gracey's Funeral Home when she told them she wanted the headstone engraved and installed now. They didn't know what to say."

"Yeah, they thought I was a little crazy but whatever." Abigail grinned and lifted her own rose from her grave. The only thing missing from her headstone was the date of her death. But that would come in due time.

"I'm finally content. And I wish you could all stay here with me forever, but I'll take as many of these visits as you'll give me. I promise to take care of the house, to keep our legacy alive until I pass. And who knows, maybe we'll be reunited on the other side sooner than I expect. You never know when your number will be called."

"Don't talk like that," Constance said. "We like how peaceful things are on the other side. Stay over here as long as you can."

The sound of their laughter filled the cemetery, echoing off the trees and headstones and spurring a flock of starlings to take flight. As they laughed, Abigail felt simultaneously relieved and frustrated. She wanted this reunion to last forever, to be with them indefinitely. Death seemed to promise a gift she'd never have in life–an eternity of love and family. While it was true she'd planned her funeral so it would be properly handled, she'd had other motivations, ones she wouldn't admit to her family.

She hoped that day would come sooner, not later.

She longed to finally have peace. To have *her* day in the flow, *her* awakening in the afterlife.

Abigail's life, while precious, would be difficult. No matter how many floorboards she replaced or walls she painted, she'd spend the rest of her life in that house, reliving those moments, constantly enduring the memories staining the house's fibers. She'd make it through the vivid memories, but she *would* experience them.

Every death.

Every nightmarish dream and vision.

Every wet footprint, *every night*.

The thrashing in the tub.

The screaming, heartbroken women of the Whispering House, there one moment, then gone the next.

The fires raging in the sitting room. Her sister's death on a loop.

Her mind spiraled back to that night in her bedroom, when Shadow Mother tempted her into the open casket and filled her with lies and false promises. She heard that calm, raspy voice in her ears again.

Enter the flow and drink deeply.

And she had. Abigail had accepted her fate that night, willingly welcomed death. But it wasn't her time. And now she had to wait until that time came.

And the waiting burned.

When her time finally came, she'd open her mouth and inhale the flow like a woman stranded in a desert. She'd drink it until her stomach refused to take more. And she'd do it with a tremendous sense of relief because she'd finally be with her loved ones again. No haunting memories needed.

Sometimes, the thought of living without the laughing faces before her felt like too much to bear. Then, she'd remember what Lydia once said to Constance, and she'd remind herself she could live with and for those memories now. She could be with them through the haunting. And that would have to be enough.

She'd repeat Lydia's words when nothing seemed real and all she wanted was her mother's loving embrace but it couldn't be found on this side of the flow.

She'd say them to soothe her aching, her longing, her utter despair.

True love is deeper than any grave.

CHAPTER 31

CONSTANCE

Constance followed closely behind Abigail as they led the women of the Whispering House from the cemetery. They walked in silence, the weight of the afternoon's ceremonial gathering steadying their souls and inspiring introspection. Although they'd suffered tremendously on this side, the fight was over. They were free to move on.

All except for Abigail, Constance thought as she watched her sister's loose curls bounce between her shoulder blades with her steps. Ahead, the late afternoon sun straddled the roof of the home, steadily turning against the day and toward the edge of night. Soon, they approached the house, a haunted pile of wood and nails, plaster and paint.

Abigail had convinced Constance to live with her in the home after they'd banished Shadow Mother and liberated Mallory, Grace, Cora, and Clara to the afterlife. But no matter how many floorboards they replaced or walls they painted, Constance couldn't avoid the smell of her burning flesh. Her blood ran through the joists, into the foundation, and pulsed through the walls. Their death saturated the fibers of the house down to the soil.

Here, where the living dwelled, the unfortunate dead remained with their sorrows tethering them to the past like a rusting, immovable anchor grounding a ship to the same rocky shoals that breached its hull. In the house, her sorrows spoke to her in constant whispers, reminding her of every lost dream, every destroyed relationship. And in the center of it all, Abigail drifted from room to room in a determined spell, her mood solemn and draped in grief. Seeing her like that destroyed Constance.

She deserves so much more. A better life. Not this.

They all did. But only Abigail still had a life to live.

•

Evening overtook the sky above the backyard like high tide washing footprints and children's sandcastles into the sea. Constance sat beside Abigail in the center of the yard, their fingers inches apart in the grass behind them as they craned their faces up to the night's stars. The others had returned to the afterlife before the moon climbed the horizon, leaving Constance to her choices on this side of death.

"Hello, Orion." Abigail grinned up at the bold constellation spanning the sky. Constance loved how Abigail always found him before she did.

"Today was nice." Constance tipped her head toward Abigail's until they met, crown to crown.

"It truly was. I think the ladies liked their flowers."

"They definitely did. Thanks for setting things right for everyone." Constance tried but failed to keep her sadness from modulating her words and catching Abigail's attention.

"It was an emotional day," Abigail said, presumably to settle her.

"Aren't they all?"

Abigail twisted her body toward Constance. "Hey. Are you okay?"

Constance kept her eyes on the stars. "No."

"What is it?"

Constance let her watery eyes shift from the stars to the trees gently swaying like drunken giants against the twinkling backdrop.

"Hey. Look at me. What's up?"

Constance met her gaze. "This isn't right, Abi. You feel it. I see it every time you greet the morning with a sigh instead of a smile. You're drowning and I can't save you."

Abigail's pressed lips quaked. Tears slowly filled her eyes. But she didn't deny Constance's claims. She couldn't deny the truth.

"When I'm here on this side, the house feels—sour. Like spoiled milk sliding down my throat. But over there, it's beautiful. It's perfect, Abi. But not here. This place is wrong for the dead."

A desperate breath slowly seeped past Abigail's parted, quivering lips. "Please, Connie. Don't—"

"I'm holding you back," Constance finally said. She felt like she'd tipped over the edge of a towering cliff. Let the valley floor below speed up and end her pain.

"But...I need you." Abigail sounded youthful, like she did at Constance's hospital bedside all those years ago.

"I—*we*—fought so hard to keep you here so you could *live*. That can't happen with me, a literal ghost, clinging to you," Constance said.

"That's not true. You're...you're all I've got." Abigail's quiet sobs nearly kept her from finishing her sentence.

"I shouldn't have let this go for so long. I'm supposed to be your protector. Instead, *you* protected me from acknowledging my death all those years."

"I'm sorry, I shouldn't have lied to you. But that doesn't mean you have to leave."

Constance took Abigail's hands in hers to silence her opposition. "Chasing the dead isn't living, Abi. I watch you chase our past every day. Those memories with Mama, with me, with all of us—they're yours forever. You're not destroying the past by moving on, you're creating a life. You'll never find a life in the bloody fabric of our past."

"But I can't be alone. No one in this town wants me." Abigail wiped her tears with her sleeve.

Constance pointed at herself, then at her sister. "But this is not the answer, Abi. Make friends. Find someone to love you. Have children. You deserve it more than anyone I've ever known." Constance stood and helped Abigail up from the grass. "It's time for me to go."

There was so much more she wanted to say but her words felt insufficient. Instead, she laced her fingers in her little sister's and led her across the yard and into their childhood home for the last time.

CHAPTER 32

ABIGAIL

Abigail knew grief. The emotion had clung to her spirit for decades, never leaving, never flagging, and persistently throbbing at the edges of every heartbeat. But grieving the loss of Constance for the second time felt unbearable, biting into her with particularly sharp teeth. The kind of debilitating pain that took the words from her mouth, the breath from her lungs.

None of it compared to the heartache she felt as the quiet house took them in. The single bulb above the kitchen table greeting them with bands of dim yellow light. After sitting under the night sky, the light, which used to comfort her, antagonized her vision. Moving away from the light and into the darker reaches of the house, Constance glided from the kitchen toward the hall, the flow pulling her like a magnet. Undeniable and unrelenting.

"We don't have to do this, Connie. You can stay. We'll figure out how to make it work."

Without responding, Constance led her sister to the stairs, their fingers interlaced. Abigail stared at their hands guiding her through the house, one a solid, living, blood-filled hand and the other a ghostly appendage. Constance's words in the yard rang like a tuning fork in her memory.

This place is wrong for the dead. It's time for me to go.

Her mind screamed at her to fight against this decision, to convince Constance to stay. To beg her to change her mind and commit to waiting with her for the day she *finally* left this ugly, empty place for the joyous, loving home her deceased loved ones inhabited.

This wretched house—but beautiful.

When they reached the stairs, Constance paused, looking down at the first step.

Without a word, she started their final ascent together.

"Connie..." Abigail stumbled on the first step, her unwilling feet feeling distant, detached.

"We have to do this," Constance replied, keeping her head forward.

Abigail knew she wouldn't stop. Stopping would give Abigail a chance to quit, to argue, to continue living as they had. Constance needed to move them forward, make the hard decision, then carry through.

The stairs disappeared beneath them. At the top of the landing, Abigail pulled to the right, toward her room. Perhaps she could stall there. To convince Constance to lay with her one last time. She'd rather fall asleep in her sister's arms and wake alone than witness her departure.

But Constance wouldn't allow it.

"Abi, I want you there. I want you to send me home."

Constance's words, concise and direct, said so much. Abigail's emotions soared. *This* was home. Why did she have to go? But deep down, Abigail knew why.

Salty tears poured from her eyes and down her cheeks as she nodded. She understood. Constance wasn't leaving this house, she was leaving her sister.

"Please." Constance turned and pulled Abigail into the dark void across the hall.

Into the bathroom.

Abigail reached in the dark for the light switch but Constance pressed her arm down.

"No. They'll make your dreams worse. Keep them off."

"Okay." It's all Abigail could manage despite the torrent of desperate words raging through her mind.

Constance reached past her and opened the door enough to give the room its shadows. Beside them, the tub waited, full and gently roiling.

It's hungry, Abigail thought. *It's always hungry.*

Constance lifted one shaky foot and stopped, her lips silently moving without sound. Abigail prayed she would change her mind, drop her foot to the floor instead of the tub. She'd rip Constance away from the tub, away from the perilous edge of eternity, and they'd fall into the hall together, squeezing each other tight.

She'd never let go.

"Thank you, Abi," Constance lowered her foot into the water.

Abigail's heart sank into her feet, and her panic climbed as she watched Constance lower to a seated position in the tub.

It's happening. Stop this!

Abigail collapsed to her knees beside the tub, her body a loose, pliable mass of useless bone and muscle in the face of her fear.

"Come closer," Constance said, twisting her body to lean toward the tub's edge. The water bubbled and churned around her arms. Abigail imagined Constance's legs dangling just above the current, moments from the flow whisking her away.

Abigail swayed on her knees like a mindless statue.

Constance pulled her closer, their fingers still intertwined, and kissed her full on the lips. "*Live.*"

They pressed their cheeks together, then their foreheads, Abigail nodding. "I will."

"Good. I'll be watching," Constance warned, a sly sisterly smile pulling her lips up at one end.

Their faces parted, Constance's spectral kiss lingering on her lips. Helpless, Abigail watched Constance slide into the water, their fingers still locked together.

An inhuman groan tumbled through Abigail's chest as the water's frenzy commenced. Constance's limbs, barely visible through the tumultuous surface in the dark, loosely danced like a puppet at the hands of a marionette. Vibrations radiated up through their clasped hands, shaking Abigail into awareness. Water soaked her clothes and splashed her face, spilling to the floor. The sound of crashing waves reverberated from the tiles, piercing and violent.

Through it all, Abigail heard that animalistic groan in her chest and throat, the vocal manifestation of her grief.

She tried to pull Constance back to her, but the opposing force held her just below the water's surface.

They were at the precipice.

One of them had to let go.

Constance looked up through the water, squeezed Abigail's hand once, and mouthed the words *I love you,* before she loosened her grip.

Tears falling into the water between them, Abigail mouthed the words *I love you, too,* then unclasped her fingers from her sister's and gently pushed Constance into eternity.

Into the *flow.*

To the afterlife.

To eternal peace.

To the home she'd always deserved.

WHAT'S NEXT?

Join the list at https://www.lucasmarinowrites.com/f or early access to new publications, exclusive content, and news. I'll never share or sell your information, and I'll never spam your inbox.

QUICK FAVOR

Thank you so much for dedicating your time to reading this book! May I ask a quick favor?

Will you please take a moment to leave a review on Goodreads and wherever you purchased the book? Your words have power. Your review can help this book reach more readers. I appreciate you!

THOUGHTS AND THANKS

You did it! You finished the series! Thank YOU for reading these stories. This last book was a tough story to write. I had *so many* goals but the challenge of pulling the final act together was brutal. The story wanted to fly once I introduced Cora and Mallory but they weren't the reason for Act III. We (I?) needed resolution. I knew that that looked like in concept but execution is a whole other game. We had a saying in the military: No plan survives first contact with the enemy. That certainly held true with this book as the chapters slowly came together and the picture became more clear. I'm grateful for Zach's patience and guidance which had a huge impact on the formulation of the final three chapters and helped me land this story.

Truthfully, I wasn't sure where the women of the Whispering House would take us but I think they made respectable decisions, regardless of how we wanted this to end. But do stories every truly end? Abigail's certainly isn't over and the others are all starting their...after...lives? Please don't assume I'm hinting at another book in the series—I'm most definitely *not*. But have faith that these characters, who are very much alive in our hearts and imaginations, exist beyond these pages because you've given them life. Without you reading their stories, they wouldn't exist. They'll live between us. And with any luck, we'll avoid the grief, the loss, the longing, and the Mother because of their sacrifices. But I welcome their love, Constance's fire, Abigail's resilience, and Adeline's wit. To think this whole thing started with that little girl and the terrible tragedy Lydia endured.

So, now I get to share a brief glimpse into *Bury the Child* and Lydia's theme. She embodied a perception of mourning that I've often contemplated but am terrified to experience. Loss is inevitable in our lives. *We lose loved ones.* But Lydia experiences an unbearable grief that comes with an unexpected beauty, a spiritual reunion that leads to her joining Adeline in her final resting place. To me, their story, their reunion is the most meaningful part of this entire series. While much of this series was written to entertain you, Lydia's story was written to make you think. Although she found an unrivaled beauty in Adeline's bedroom after the funeral, a grieving experience beyond what any of us expect, there is no comparison to the love we share in our lives together. Live for each other. Love!

Speaking of love, none of his would be possible without the support of my wife, Tammie. Thank you for helping me work through a million ideas, good and bad, to finally close this series. You saved these characters so many times I lost count. I love you.

Caleb, Gabriel, and Madelyn – You kids keep me young(-ish). Without your love and ridiculousness, I wouldn't have the heart or energy to write. I love you so much. And although Caleb and Gabriel would prefer to avoid these books because I wrote them, I have faith Maddie will eventually get around to reading the last two and letting me know how "cringe" my writing is. :)

Mom and Dad – Thanks for always asking how the book was coming along and for helping me build the bookshop in the final month of writing this book. Doesn't your son always have the best timing? You always put us first. I love you!

A top team of professionals supported this novel, starting with my friend and editor, Zach Bohannon. Thanks for the constant guidance, Zach. Working with you on this series was a blessing. Thanks for pushing me to sharpen this story and really stick the landing. This book is unquestionably better thanks to your guidance.

Clarissa Yeo is the talent behind the book cover art and Drew Huff is the magician who designed the cover wrap. I thank you both for dedicating your artistic talents to this book! Clarissa, I wish you great luck in your new career! And Drew, thanks for coming through for me in a pinch. I owe you one.

Finally, I extend my sincere thanks to the friends and readers following this series via my email newsletters. If you stuck around long enough to read this and you're finding out about the newsletter for the first time, join us at www.lucasmarinowrites.com ! We can exchange emails like pen pals. If you're ever in Williamsburg, come by my bookshop, Spineless Reads, and say hi!

ABOUT THE AUTHOR

Lucas writes thriller, suspense, and horror fiction. If he's not writing, he's reading, playing guitar, or enjoying time with his family. Lucas is also the owner of Spineless Reads fiction bookstore in Williamsburg, VA, the host of *The Suspense is Killing Me* podcast, and cofounder of Sobelo Books, an indie publisher of dark speculative fiction.

A military engineer by experience, he spent twenty-one years in the United States Coast Guard. He earned his Doctor of Engineering and Master of Science degrees in Engineering Management and Systems Engineering at The George Washington University.

He now lives in a pile of trees in Virginia.

MUSICAL INSPIRATION

- David Gilmour (with Romany Gilmour) - Between Two Points
  As with *Bless the Mother*, this was my top listen while writing this book.

- Peter Gabriel – Love Can Heal (Dark Side Mix)

- Agents of Oblivion – Hangman's Daughter

- Pink Floyd – High Hopes

- Porcupine Tree – Anestetize

- Porcupine Tree – Arriving Somewhere But Not Here

- Opeth – A Story Never Told

- Tesseract – Tourniquet

- Fleetwood Mac – Beautiful Child

- Jinjer – Perennial

- Charlotte Martin – Cloudbursting (Studio)

- Ursine Vulpine – One Last Moment Of You

- Garbage – The Trick Is To Keep Breathing

- Manequin Pussy – Loud Bark

- Persona – All For You

- The Fire Theft – Waste Time

- Sparta – While Oceana Sleeps

- Sparta – Erase It Again

- Spiritbox – Constance

- Deftones – Entombed

- Deftones – Digital Bath

- Leprous – The Sky Is Red

- Periphery – Reptile

- Radiohead - Street Spirit (Fade Out)

- Tori Amos – Lieee

- Tori Amos – Night Of Hunters (Sin Palabras)

- Violent Femmes – Color Me Once